BOOKING IN THE HEARTLAND

Jack Matthews

BOOKING

in the

HEARTLAND

The Johns Hopkins University Press
Baltimore and London

The Johns Hopkins University Press
701 West 40th Street
Baltimore, Maryland 21211
The Johns Hopkins Press Ltd., London

∞

*The paper used in this publication meets the minimum requirements
of American National Standard for Information Sciences—
Permanence of Paper for Printed Library Materials, ANSI Z39.48-1984.*

Library of Congress Cataloging-in-Publication Data
Matthews, Jack.
Booking in the heartland.

Matthews, Jack.   2. Book collectors—United States—Biography.
3. Book collecting—United States.   4. Rare books—
Collectors and collecting.   I. Title.
Z989.M3A32   1986   002′.075′0924 [B]   86-7150
ISBN 0-8018-3332-9 (alk. paper)

Some of these essays originally appeared in *Adena, The Cresset, The Ohio Magazine,* and *The Ohioana Quarterly* (copyrighted 1983 by the Martha Kinney Cooper Ohioana Library Association). "Books and Learning on the Old Frontier, God Help Us" was read at the opening ceremonies for the Hocking Technical College Museum on May 16, 1981; "Wasting Time" was read before the Caxton Club of Chicago on October 20, 1982; and "New Opportunities in Old Books" was originally—in somewhat different form—a talk before the Ohio Library Media Association in Cincinnati on November 2, 1985.

TO BOB ROE
a booking pal for, lo, these many years.

Contents

Preface

Booking in the Heartland is largely a book of memoirs, therefore both personal and philosophical, because memoirs are an attempt to connect one's individual lot and character with the larger ideas, values, truths, prejudices, and validities that loom over the world.

As a book of memoirs pretty much restricted to adventures in booking (i.e., the seeking out and acquiring of old and rare books), *Booking in the Heartland* strives to be informative and anecdotal. The informative part is obvious in a context that is centered upon the book, the essential instrument of information since the birth of general literacy. As for the anecdote, it is the ordered and purposive account toward which all human events yearn . . . as even now, in the small box of this preface.

But prefaces are not the place for anecdotes, and that is their major failing. However, as signposts that point toward what has been attempted and perhaps achieved, they are useful; and insofar as this book proves successfully anecdotal, it will prove not simply useful, but—to the collector and lover of rare books—something more.

BOOKING IN THE HEARTLAND

Wasting Time

Everyone's life is an evasion. We are all naturally haunted by the lives unlived, the experiences unavailable, the crises not savored. This natural sense of more-or-less chronic deprivation is intensified by the media, which provide relentless samples of relevance and importance to beguile and frustrate the majority, whose hours are wasted in assembly lines, accounting offices, and beauty shops.

That our lives are inevitably, essentially, evasions is a simple notion and even has proverbial and epigrammatic connections: "The grass is always greener on the other side of the fence" and "Heard melodies are sweet, but those unheard are sweeter." These point toward a familiar, even obvious truth; and yet, the failure to attend to it is surely the cause of much of the world's misery, especially in media-ridden cultures, where glamorized, intensified, speeded-up versions of one's necessarily unlived lives are constantly flashed before the eyes or rhymed into the ears.

We catch what we can, do what we have to do, let this go and take that up, and time slips through us without a sound. Caught up in the machinery of particular tasks at particular times, we pause often enough to ask what in the hell we're *doing*—what it's all about, how (to change the figure) we can kick the traces and go somewhere and really *live*.

I don't think anyone can escape this unnerving, at times demoralizing inference. We are free of it only when we are "caught up" in something, as the expression has it: caught up in our work or some form of pleasure. But our work is dedicated, more often than not, to obscure goals; we labor in immeasurably great castles of bureaucracy, which prove—the instant we step back and look at them—to be built upon the sands of convention and precedent, seldom evaluated. And most of our pleasures are as mindless and prove ultimately as empty as opening an outboard motor to full throttle and speeding to some other end of a lake that upon our arrival doesn't look any different from the shore we just left.

What we are driven to is the conclusion that we have been wasting time. Wasting time can be fun while it's happening, or absorbing while we're spending our life energy on a design for a new bicycle mount for a car or a method for selling more boxes of a new breakfast cereal . . . but there are interludes of sobriety (often at three in the morning), when we question the value of all this furious energy—the *point* of it—or the fundamental indignity of broadcasting our minutes and hours upon the barren ground of popular (i.e., socially prescribed) values and pleasures.

These are moments of truth, always. We do in fact spend much of our lives wasting time. Even when we labor earnestly. The Secretary of State, trying to preserve peace in various parts of the world—going without sleep, advocating mightily in the halls of arbitration for dimly understood ends and goals . . . what can such a person in the midst of the choreography of protocol understand about the miracle of living inside a skin and looking out upon a world? Even such as these must have their moments when the grass does in truth look greener somewhere else, and upon occasion they must sense the possibility, at least, of unheard melodies that might resound in the head of another, whom the media and/or the world will never know about. But, of course, whoever is living in that other head will, under scrutiny, prove to be missing out, too.

Wasting time. We all do it and, in one sense, do it constantly. You've wasted your time reading this, according to whole sets of perfectly respectable and valid principles. As have I, therefore, in writing it.

A subject of such dignity and power deserves a closer scrutiny. This much is obvious, and in the immediate context, at least, it won't be a waste of time to investigate further what the term might mean and how it can be said that virtually all that we do is, in one way or other, wasting time. And beyond that, how we can come to some sort of terms with this profoundly unsettling notion.

And ultimately, beyond *that*, to give testimony upon the subject of how I personally have managed to waste so much time in my life, which I think I can claim without boasting is far greater in sheer quantity—hours, days, and weeks—than most people can lay claim to. And *this* testimony will explain what the following book is all about.

Wasting time isn't just any sort of idea: it is an inference, a conclusion, a judgment. Therefore, it is a function of values, which means it is inextricably tangled up in the question of ends and means. Furthermore, the question of ends and means is a transactional unity—we can't have one without the other.

Wisdom has always favored the Golden Mean, ever since Aristotle (and the Greeks generally) gave lip service to it. If you spend too much time laboring at the means for something (security, comfort, wealth, even "happiness"), you will eventually be judged to have wasted your time. Not just Henry David Thoreau will come to this conclusion, but you yourself will begin to suspect it and eventually be haunted by it.

Contrarily, if you frolic your days away in sybaritic dalliance, you will eventually detect the poisonous seepage of waste into those long hours of corrupted leisure. What are you *doing* with your life? What are you producing? What *good* are you? These are all accusations from that part of us that believes it is right and meaningful that we be useful, which means we take upon ourselves the discipline, dignity, and foresight to work at means.

You will recognize the ancient ethical lesson featuring the grasshopper and the ant. Contrary to the obvious and customary interpretations of the fable, however, most of us today would judge that the most useful life (the least wasted) would comprise a synthesis of the dialectic extremes symbolized by the grasshopper and the ant. Everybody should have a little of each inside, ready for the right, the timely, expression. Who wants to go to a party of ants? They ruin more than picnics. And who would want to build an ark with a shipbuilding crew of grasshoppers bopping fecklessly about while the rain falls and the water keeps rising?

What we need is some kind of synthesis, incorporating the unique genius of each mode, each attitude. Travis McGee, the detective hero of John D. MacDonald's series of color-coded novels, has devised his own formula: posing as a "salvage consultant," he takes his retirement in installments, whenever his bank account is fattened by a successful case. (This is easier to do when you are single, as McGee is, and still easier when you are a fictional character.)

We are familiar with the cautionary examples of both sorts of excess: the man who slaves all his life at a particular job, and then retires to find out he has nothing to think about; or the (less common) old-fashioned wastrel who goes through an inherited fortune in "practically no time" and suddenly finds himself "without means." Wasting time, each in his own way.

But then, not even the shrewd and wise synthesizer is totally exempt from this dark knowledge. There is always some untested part of ourselves which we can never know. There are all those things we might have done, but didn't; and all those unlived lives populate our reflective moments in postures of silent accusation. Part of this derives from the fact that as symbol users we are constantly in the presence of absence—which sounds like an Irish bull but is true enough to make us antsy, anyway. Symbols are vessels for all those impalpable things that we can't experience directly, sensuously, in themselves. Thus, they carry the past and the future, as well as those grandiose abstractions—truth, justice, beauty, and, at one time, the *Primum Mobile*. And since our heads are always filled with them, some part of otherness is always present in our lives.

So, unlike the mourning dove and the terrier, we live chronically with evidence of what we might be doing, or where we might be, but aren't. It's no wonder life is interesting. Wasting time.

Some people, however, manage to waste time with a certain dedication, a higher seriousness, even a certain panache. Some people seem to work at it in such a way that it isn't always clear that they actually *are* wasting time, or—if they are—exactly how this is being done and what its implications are. I believe that I am one of these people who waste time seriously, if I may say so without sounding boastful; and I produce the following evidence to support my claim.

I put an average of 30,000 miles per year on my car, traveling to country auctions, yard sales, junk stores, book stores in distant cities, book fairs, and antique shows. My wife and I live much of our lives in our car, a sort of second home—one that moves and uses gas and requires periodic oil changes. Thousands of miles on the large interstate highways that all look pretty much the same (although they are beautiful among wooded hills—products of a civilization that is far from being all bad), thousands of miles on back roads, nosing for caches of old books in sheds or attics and for the occasional rarity found in a junk store or antique shop.

Recently, in the mountains of western Virginia my wife and I saw an "Antiques" sign and stopped at a most unpromising place. It was an abandoned filling station, now given over to a sparse collection of miscellaneous old objects. Inside, three people were sitting, evidently surprised, if not somewhat alarmed, at our coming in. It was as nearly vacant a shop as I've ever visited, but there were long rows of wooden shelving extending the length of the store. On these shelves were fifteen or twenty books lying on their sides, along with a motley of dishes, rusty old farm and household implements, and a forlorn assemblage of pottery and mismatched jelly glasses.

The books were dirty, worn, and utterly devoid of interest . . . *except for one*. This was a copy of Thomas Birch's *The Virginian Orator*, published in Richmond in 1808. It was in the original calf binding, in excellent condition. I looked at the Table of Contents and saw that, in contrast to the popular rhetorics of that time, this book did not consist of eighteenth-century translations of the classic orations of Cicero, Quintilian, Demosthenes, et al., but was rather a compendium of contemporary speeches, beginning with Governor Hull's address to the Indians in Michigan Territory, followed by the reply of Nanuame, the Pottawatamie chief. Some of the orations are Birch's own, but most are of his contemporaries, including one by Thomas Jefferson, titled "Difference of Opinion Advantageous in Religion."

This copy was priced at $9.50, which seemed surprisingly high under the circumstances. One-fiftieth of that amount would have been more likely; and fifty times that amount would have been more valid in terms of the book's potential value.

But I didn't want the proprietor to feel bad (it was one of the women), so I asked if she couldn't take less for the book, and she replied that I could have it for $8.00. I paused briefly and then nodded. If I had paid the $9.50 without question, she would have been left wondering how badly she had underpriced the book; my saving $1.50 had at the same time provided her with what would likely be considered evidence that the book was priced more or less accurately.

Later, when I researched this 1808 sextodecimo I'd bought for $8.00 (the number eight seems to have a mystic connection with the adventure), I found it not listed in the *British Museum Catalogue* but liberally represented in the *National Union Catalogue* with references to seven (not eight) copies in various institutions, extending from the predictable (William and Mary, University of Virginia, and the Virginia State Historical Society in Richmond) to the unexpected (Brooklyn Public Library). But in spite of this generous supply, no copy of the Richmond 1808 edition was recorded as being sold at auction in the past twenty years. However, a copy of the Lexington (Ky.) 1823 reprint had sold for $100 in 1975. It appears that my cherishing this book is more than idiosyncrasy, and that my $8 purchase will prove to be one of those investments that transcend the quotidian values of the market place and shine in the memory.

The rarity and value of *The Virginian Orator* are fairly certain, though its precise dollar value may be difficult to place. It is different from books of relatively established value, such as certain private press titles. By calculation, artistry, and demand, a Doves Press, Nonesuch, or Golden Cockerel title can be as accurately priced as any class of rare book. They have been printed in limited, numbered quantities, and their track records at auction and bookshop are usually consistent and predictable.

But there is a class of book even more inscrutable than the identified rarity, and there is no greater adventure for the bibliophile than to come upon one of these. Providing, that is, it has something other than its utter scarcity or inscrutability to recommend it. Preferably, it should be either immensely readable or contain otherwise inaccessible information.

One such book that I've caught in my nets provides a clue to its peculiarity on the title page:

RIBS AND TRUCKS,
From Davy's Locker;
being
MAGAZINE MATTER BROKE LOOSE,
and
FRAGMENTS OF SUNDRY THINGS IN-EDITED.
By W.A.G.

Below this, there is a horizontal bar, and then "Boston: / Charles D. Strong. / 1842." The copyright was issued in Strong's name the same year. Probably a first edition.

But first edition of what? "Ribs and Trucks" is an old nautical term for a miscellany of fragments, "bits and pieces." Not too surprising a title for a small, 199-page volume of essays and poems.

The first chapter is titled "A Chapter on Whaling" and bears on epigraph from *The Tempest*. After this, the reader is launched upon an astonishing flood of rhetoric, beginning thus:

WHALING! And what, O what, cries the reader, (thrice critical and captious personage,) can there be in connection with whaling, the bare mention of which leaves not a palpable greasespot on the hitherto unsullied pages of Maga?[1] We are not in the "oil line," and take comparatively little interest in the light-engendering speculations of our neighbors of the "treeless isle;" so pr'ythee, spare us thy spermaceti statistics. Placid reader, if such be your ejaculation, permit me to say, you are unwarrantably raw to the romance of the subject. 'Tis high time you were aware that few voyages, at least, can boast of greater attractions than a "whaling cruise" offers to the nautical lounger, the novelty hunter, the devotee of exciting sports—the anything, or anybody, in short, in any manner "wedded to the imperial sea." 'Tis your whaler alone, who goes down *to* the sea, in ships; other mariners hurry across it. He alone does business *upon* the great waters; and, more emphatically than other "seafarers," makes the ocean his home. With his top-sail-yard "sharp up," and his helm "four spokes alee," he rides out the storm, month in and month out—nesting, like a sea bird, in the trough, and feeling himself, as it were, in harbor; while other ships rise on the horizon, and scud by, and lessen and reel out of sight, with blind celerity, on their respective courses. A trip to Europe may serve to introduce the novice to the "blue deity," but, for a thorough acquaintance, commend me to the long, familiar intercourse of a whaling voyage.

"Art quite asleep?—if not, follow we yonder sea-seasoned vessel, a few thousand miles, to her frolicking-place in the Southern ocean. Were she a "Cape Horner," the favor of your company were too much to ask; but her cruise is to end in nine months; and she shall confine herself to our own Atlantic—or straying thence, it shall be only for a few months, "beyond the Cape of Hope." . . .

Surely, thought I upon reading this (having been infected by its style), 'tis none other than a passage from Herman Melville's *magnum opus*, which at that time lay fomenting in the vat of history, awaiting its full cycle to be tapped, bottled, and corked in the great octavo the world knows as *Moby Dick!* So (to step outside that style)

1. New England Magazine

I did some checking. Could W.A.G. have been Melville himself, practicing his flourishes nine years before his great masterpiece was launched?

But this would appear to be impossible, for Melville had sailed on a whaling ship on January 1, 1841, and stayed aboard until the next summer, when he took his famous leave-without-absence and ended up living with savages in the Typee valley. So he had to have been somewhere in the South Seas when *Ribs and Trucks* was copyrighted and published, for he didn't reach civilization until 1843.

Could he have written the book before sailing? Not likely: the essay reads as a personal testament, all the way through, and it seems wildly improbable that Melville could have dashed off this enthusiasm in the very manner of *Moby Dick*, totally inexperienced in whaling, and nine years before the great book itself was published, especially considering the tardiness of his development as a writer.

Finding antecedent influences upon *Moby Dick* was the rage of "relevant scholarship" a generation ago, and there are possibly even some undergraduates today who know about J. N. Reynolds's "Mocha Dick; or, The White Whale," which had appeared in *The Knickerbocker Magazine* in May, 1839. There is also the undeniable influence of Carlyle, whose thundrous style is now hardly a murmur in the deepest stacks of out-dated libraries.

But none of these previous works, with all their influences, comes together as it does here. If highly sophisticated readers of English prose who have not read Melville's grandiose masterpiece could be found somewhere, I think the opening chapter of *Ribs and Trucks* could be inserted in Melville's text and it would turn with the gears of the novel without a squeak in their hearing.

The likeness is more than astonishing: it is uncanny. This resemblance has more than what is usually meant by "style": the argument is *conceived* as Melville conceived it, as is evident in that sentence that states: "'Tis your whaler alone, who goes down *to* the sea, in ships; other mariners hurry across it." Melville utters the same thought, in the same terms; but he does so less tersely, as if troubled by vague memories that, somehow, somewhere, this exact idea has been expressed before. Had he read, assimilated, and forgotten W.A.G.'s essay? Or did he remember it very well, knowing a good thing when he heard it?

We don't have to choose between these alternatives—there's too little evidence to go on. The great omission is the identity of W.A.G.,

whose initials seem to mock us waggishly. I have checked the obvious references, haunted by the suspicion that this was a humorous
acronym only pretending to be initials, and have found absolutely
nothing that fits the time and place.

The *British Museum Catalogue* does not list *Ribs and Trucks* at all,
but *The National Union Catalogue* lists copies at Harvard, Chicago,
Philadelphia, and Buffalo. I have written to all of these libraries,
and all have answered my inquiries. None of them has the least
notion of who W.A.G. might have been.

For a while, I trifled with the idea that it might have been Dr. W.
A. Greenhill, an English physician. His dates are right, and he
might have had a two-year adventure on an American whaler. But
after tracking down his obituary in the *The Atheneum* (Sept. 29,
1894), I realized that this was not possible.

So we are left with nothing, an absence, a mystery, three meaningless initials. I phoned the U.S. Copyright Office, and was told I
could hire a clerk at $10 an hour to seek out the identity of the
author of *Ribs and Trucks,* if his name is in fact listed in the copyright register. However, I was also informed that copyrights can be,
or could at that time be, issued to pseudonyms or initials—a most
exasperating protection of privacy where it isn't needed. At least, I
don't need it now, almost a century and a half after the publication
of this elusive and fascinating book.

Six weeks of silence followed my receipt and submission of the
proper research form, along with a ten-dollar check, and then I
wrote again. (The telephone line at the Library of Congress is *never*
free; this is one of the world's few absolutes.) Within a week, I
received a polite and apologetic call from an official in the Copyright Office. He told me there had been a mistake; copyrights made
before 1870 simply do not exist in the Copyright Office. Somewhere
in the silence surrounding this man's voice, I heard a snicker. It was
not the copyright official who'd snickered; it was Wag; and I swear
he sounded a little like Bartleby the Snickerer, as he might have
sounded if he'd ever *not* preferred not to.

As for my caller, he was not only concerned but interested, and
said he would see if there were other means for seeking out the
right, true author of *Ribs and Trucks.* For which I thanked him. So
that now the matter still rests in that limbo. And while I am waiting, not too hopefully, for this report, I can brood over the old ink
inscription on the front flyleaf of my copy:

Presented to Mrs. Whittelsey
By her friend
Mrs. Horace Greely

In spite of the apparently missing "e" from the second syllable, could this be *the* Mrs. Horace Greeley? Chronology allows it; Greeley was married in 1836 and stayed married for a long time after *Ribs and Trucks* was evidently forgotten. Is it possible that W.A.G. was Greeley himself? Well, what do you do with the first two initials? Furthermore, Greeley had no middle initial, even if you somehow rationalize the conversion of the "H" into a "W"; *furthermore,* during this period, Greeley was about as busy as a man can be, launching the *New York Tribune,* and there is no evidence that Greeley knew anything, or cared much, about whaling.

So we are left with the sensed presence of a ghostly writer of a wonderfully obscure book that conveys in tone, style, and content a most remarkable preview of the most gigantic book in American literature. Not necessarily (and not necessarily *not*) the best, or greatest (our vocabulary doesn't allow for such precisions as these words suggest), but surely the most gigantic, in subject and theme. "Give me a condor quill!" Melville says through the mouth of Ishmael. "Give me Vesuvius' crater for an inkstand! . . . to produce a mighty book, you must choose a mighty theme!"

But nine years before this, a man who signed his name "Wag," which is to say, "Joker" or "Trickster," wrote a piece that shows he had dipped the same quill in the same ink; however, it is only the uncanny essay that has survived, along with the jesting name; as for the man himself, he has gone the way of all those whalers who had real names in a real time, but out of their anonymity helped provide the great cosmic metaphor for Melville's book.

These adventures are the sort all book collectors take joy in telling about, just as they rejoice in hearing similar accounts from other collectors. There is a romance to such finds that is unique to book collecting, in my view, because the prize is so potent a symbol that there is nothing conceivable that cannot be figured in it. What is there in this world or beyond which can't be thought of as casting a shadow of print on a white page?

Wasting time? Surely not, after "striking it rich" in that dark and dirty little room that had once been part of a filling station! *The Virginian Orator* proved a splendid harvest after so many hours of driving. This "long cut" that paralleled the interstate highway was picturesque, of course, but slower than the interstate, and even the picturesque grows familiar and banal with time.

How many "finds" do I need per thousand miles or per hundred hours to keep searching? And of what magnitude? A first edition of Thomas Wolfe's *Of Time and the River* would have been welcome at $8.00. In fine condition, with dust jacket, cause for rejoicing; signed by Wolfe (we were not far from Asheville), considerably more rejoicing; inscribed, even more . . . but independent of market value, the prize would still not be as great as that which I did in fact chance upon.

Things become complicated, and clear judgments are difficult to arrive at, even though in a sense, we are forced to make them anyway. Often in retrospect I look back and think: *Right then, I was about to give up and call it a day, but just before quitting I came upon this copy of . . .*

But I know I am fooling myself. Because my patience is flexible and stretches to hours and even days in one context before the great compensatory find, and seems to have been immanent after an hour on another occasion when a rare or desirable title swims to the surface in some stew of miscellaneous volumes.

I know that I am playing a game with myself, partly unaware. I don't measure the time of searching—the long, dull hours in the car, driving, or the tedious hours pawing through boxes of books or squatting before shelves, tracing my index fingers along spines and forcing myself to take in what I'm looking at. What I am really measuring is the intervals between the finds themselves; that is, *they* serve as temporal units, while conventional time (which we have learned is relative) beats out its own irrelevant measure. This explains how two hours can be utterly absorbed in looking at lots of books I haven't seen before, and those two hours can fit inside a thimble of minutes (ask my wife, who sits in the car and reads while she waits—she'll tell you).

And thus, the time wasted is of a different dimension entirely, and the count, along with the wastage, is altered.

This game is not totally of my own devising, however. Part of it merges into superstition. By "superstition" I don't refer to an attitude that is necessarily invalid or untrue: I simply mean a feeling that can't be precisely articulated and is not subject to the laws of empirical fact.

BOOKING IN THE HEARTLAND

Most book collectors of my acquaintance, and probably most book scouts—almost by definition—share in this superstition, which is connected with serendipity. Most serendipity has nothing to do with superstition, of course. To some extent, it is nothing more than skill in logic—the capacity for valid inductive inference, as it is most obviously manifest in generating workable hypotheses. To some extent, and in some situations, it is merely the possession of relevant information. Recently, in answer to a classified ad I'd run in the local newspaper, a woman called, saying she had a few old leather books. I drove to her house, which was situated on a back country road in the midst of rolling pasture and woodland, and found that one of these books was the 1619 Paris edition of Heliodorus's *Aethiopica* in vellum, perfectly preserved. The title page was in classical Greek and then, directly below, was translated into classical Latin. The date was, of course, in Roman numerals. It was not the sort of book I usually anticipate finding in response to such an ad, but if I hadn't been able to read the title page I would have had as little to go on as the owner had, and the element of serendipity in the transaction (yes, I bought the book) would have had to wait for another opportunity.

But there is a kind of serendipper who *senses* things. It sounds fanciful, but is utterly exact, to say that when Heliodorus's book and I were introduced, two histories converged: one of over three and a half centuries and the other somewhat less. As a book collector, I find myself verging upon a superstitious belief in signs. If I hadn't stopped at that downtrodden little erstwhile filling station in western Virginia, then I wouldn't have gotten one of the most cherished books in my collection. If you look hard enough, and search with enough energy, books seem to come alive in ways different from the metaphorical life we know they possess: they seem to come to you as much as you come to them, pretty much as you witness fence posts, telephone poles, and advertising signs approaching as you ride in a passenger car.

Foolishness, of course. At least, in a way. And yet the attitude that contains this foolishness is healthy; and ultimately, in various and unpredictable ways, effective, for it brings in more books—more to choose from and therefore more to buy selectively and, in rare moments, passionately.

So the superstitious part doesn't really bother me; in fact, it increases the enjoyment, the game aspect of booking. Such superstition doesn't even have to be defended with psychological and instrumental arguments, such as these I am expressing at this moment, for the pleasure it brings is rich with adventure.

And yet, behind it all is the realization that I am wasting time. I could be spending my hours more profitably or doing something more worthwhile. It has to be this way, as I have argued: there's no escaping it. You pay for everything, and there are few moments as desolate as those when you have spent almost an entire day driving through the countryside, looking for books—stopping at yard and garage sales, depressing little junk stores that smell of decay and cat urine, antique shops whose proprietors respond to your inquiry about books with a frozen stare . . . few moments as dispiriting, so that you are on the verge of swearing off booking forever and yet swerve sharply to pull off the road at the next sign, secretly convinced that a copy of *Alice's Adventures in Wonderland,* London, 1865, will be stuffed on a shelf between copies of an Introductory Algebra, copyrighted in 1956, and *Forever Amber.* Or perhaps it will be a first edition of *Pilgrim's Progress,* with an inscription from Bunyan, blessing whoever buys this book.

The distinction between knowledge and information is always possible but happens in different ways in different contexts. This is evident from a commonplace inscribed by a girl in her penmanship book in the 1850s. I can't remember where I purchased this old book or what else was written in it, but one sentence shines in my memory: "Ignorance of such things is part of knowledge." What "such things" were is not clear, but given the time and place, I suspect they must lie in the region of vulgarity, pointed toward sex. It is a noble and triumphant statement, in its way; and the word "information" could not conceivably be substituted for "knowledge," for the latter must clearly have an ethical character for this paradox to make sense, and it must in some way overlap what we usually mean by "wisdom."

Paraphrasing, one might say that ignorance of the laws of probability in finding astonishing rarities is part of knowledge in the pursuit of books. Here, knowledge will not translate down to "information" any more readily than it will in that anonymous girl's sentence. If I had to bet my life or all my worldly possessions on the probability of finding a rare book in even a score of antique shops or yard sales, I wouldn't be so foolish. However, the cost in time and travel is very real, and each stop and inquiry that doesn't pay off is simply the turn of another wrong card. Wasting time.

And yet, if I am paying something, I am paying *for* something, and probably no one but a gambler or a book collector could understand what this is. Ignorance of the actuarial probability is part of knowledge if prolonged and stultifying effort and expenditure lead to a treasure of whose existence you knew nothing . . . which has been the case with many titles that now help populate my library, including *Ribs and Trucks,* by a self-named Wag, and Thomas Birch's *The Virginian Orator.*

Sharp's Western Diary

**T**his is a happy story about a good, honorable, and courageous man. Indirectly, it is about his father as well, who was worthy of having such a son. There is also a villain in the story. We don't know what happened to him, but there is a happy ending to the adventures of the father and son, and everything I have learned about them is fascinating.

My information comes from a little forty-seven-page book whose title page reads:

LIFE AND DIARY
OF
ROBERT LEE SHARP

Naturalist and Geologist
Pioneer and Statesman

by
His Son
William Hale Sharp

If there is copyright data on the verso it can't be seen, because an old photo of Robert Lee Sharp, "Upon his return from California in 1854" (typed on the photo's bottom margin), covers most of the page. Nevertheless, William Hale Sharp's brief epilogue is dated "Sept. 29, 1938," and no doubt this is when the book was printed. It is bound in blue cloth with gilt lettering on the front boards (the spine is too narrow for lettering); and the back cover is badly mottled. This is one of only two copies I have ever seen (the Wagnall's

Library in Lithopolis, Ohio, has the other), but this may be due simply to the fact that only 50 or 100 copies were printed and bound. Since I've never heard anyone mention the book and have seen only one reference to it, I assume that it is not widely cherished as a rarity.

The fact is, however, it should be. Robert Lee Sharp's story is a thoroughly engrossing one, and it begins with his father, Joseph, who in 1838 "completed a dam for the improvement of the Muskingum River." William Hale Sharp's introduction continues with the astonishing revelation that, after this, Joseph "sent his commisary store, with Robert, who was then 14 years of age, to manage it, to Sugar Grove, Ohio, where it was set up in an old frame building belonging to Nicholas Beery, father of Major Elijah Beery, east of Rush Creek and Sugar Grove." (This is in Fairfield County, near Lancaster.)

That a fourteen-year-old boy should be placed in charge of such an enterprise is impressive, but Joseph's confidence was not misplaced, as the following story reveals.

This was the era of canal building, and the state of Ohio had undertaken to connect its boundaries, including Lake Erie and the Ohio River, with a network of canals. Public bonds were issued, but their sale was not great enough to subsidize the Hocking Canal. Eventually, however, several men, including Joseph Sharp, mortgaged their personal assets to float these bonds. By this time, Sharp had built several dams on the Hocking River, and had become a man of wealth and substance.

He had also taken on a partner, named Archibald McCann, and the two had contracted to build a considerable portion of the canal. The rest should be told by Joseph's grandson, who edited Robert Lee's California diary:

> Sharp and McCann were notified that if they would come to Columbus they could draw the money on their estimates of the work that had been completed. Joseph Sharp said to the younger man, "You take the horse and saddle bags and go to Columbus and draw the estimates." (This was before the days of the railway.) McCann did so, and the horse and McCann never returned. Robert's father had encumbered everything he had in order to complete the execution of the contracts, and McCann drawing this large sum of money and absconding left his father hopelessly in debt. Joseph Sharp had always paid his debts, and he and his sons worked hard at farming and quarrying stone on their land in order to pay the debts. Robert said it

was obvious to him that his father could not pay his debts without some help. Therefore, on April 19, 1852, Robert Lee Sharp, who was then 27 years of age, departed for the gold fields in California, thinking he might find enough gold to pay his father's debts. He kept a diary on his trip as far as Placerville, California.

Robert Lee Sharp was successful: he found gold and mined it. He returned home by way of the Isthmus of Panama, paid off every mortgage, married his childhood sweetheart, who had been waiting for him, and then settled down to farm the land his father had given him in return for his rescuing Joseph from financial ruin.

All of the ingredients of old-fashioned melodrama are here, excepting one: the comeuppance of the villain. So far as we can know, the perfidious McCann was never heard of again, and one hopefully contemplates the possibility that he might have died of syphilis or was eaten by wild hogs.

And why did Robert Sharp keep his diary only as far as Placerville? Because that's where he ran out of paper to write on.

"It is not growing like a tree / in size that makes man better be," Ben Jonson wrote; and as it is with mankind generally, so it is with books. Robert Lee Sharp's diary was obviously written cautiously, each entry a frugal expenditure, in view of the limited paper he had. The style is not so much laconic, as it is focused upon those essential facts abstracted from all that Sharp saw. More books should be written this way.

Not that the diary is devoid of repetition. Every grave marker Sharp encountered must have been noted. The cholera had taken its toll and was still harvesting corpses. The count of graves per day is a sort of odometer; in this regard, Sharp's account is like many others: one had to be impressed by the simple numbers of corpses populating the earth beside the trail.

What raises Sharp's account above the ordinary is the quality of his mind, which means simply that he had a sense of what made the adventure he was experiencing unique and powerful. And in truth there were astonishing things to witness, so that the greater astonishment is that so many people could have kept diaries and journals and yet failed to see so much. Consider Sharp's entry for May 17:

We crossed Little Sandy or Turkey Creek, a great many wagons crossing. There was an Indian shot here night before last for stealing a mule. We encamped one and a half miles from this stream. We saw some men returning home discouraged, and saw two carts made out of a wagon by cutting it in two, one man returning home and the other going on. We see dead steers every day lying along road. We saw one grave today.

This was an eventful day for two reasons: that extraordinary "splitting up" of a single-wagon party and the fact that only one grave was encountered. A one-grave day was uncommon. On June 8, for example, their party passed thirteen graves . . . "this year's," Sharp specifies, for the older graves had been dug up by wolves.

Elsewhere, Sharp tells an appalling and tragic story about a man who got into an argument with his son-in-law and made him, along with his daughter and their sick infant, leave his train. The child died the same day, and some men from Sharp's train buried it. As for its parents,

> They were still there this morning when we left, with very little covering. . . . A small sack of flour and a piece of meat and two cows is about their all. What a forlorn state to be in, without any place to go, without money and 300 miles from the States. They refused to take them in at the Fort / Kearney / . Whether they will have to perish or whether some emigrant will take them in, we know not. I fear this is only a foretaste of what we shall see before we get to California. I feel very unwell this afternoon. The boys are beginning to read their Testaments, sing hymns and talk on scriptural subjects. Cholera has done some of us good, at least for the present. How long it will last, time will tell. We can now see wagons across the river going up the Council Bluff Road.

What the end of this tragic and pathetic episode was is unknown. The hysteria and social fragmentation of frontier life are evident in countless anecdotes such as this, and they are astonishingly incompatible with the stereotypes that dominate our popular conceptions.

In recounting the hardships of the abandoned couple, Sharp mentions their lack of money. Poverty might seem irrelevant on the frontier, but on these early trails of the old west, it was not. Probably it never was, at any time in any place; financial solvency merely seems an irrelevancy in our pictorialization of the more dramatic aspects of pioneer life.)

There were, of course, people who exploited human need, and they could be found at every stage of the overland trail. Traders were known as "land pirates," and Sharp mentions that vinegar was "$2.00 a gallon, and other things in proportion."[1]

Other stories are told so briefly that we wish Sharp had had more paper to fill them out, or else more information. On June 17, his party traveled a good twenty-four miles. They also passed several graves, and Sharp writes: "The last one we passed was that of a man who had been murdered two days ago in cold blood. The murdered man was S. Miller, and the murderer was Lafayette Sale."

But justice was neither tardy nor hesitant, and the very next day, after crossing the La Bonta River, Sharp's party came upon Sale's grave. "He was followed by the emigrants to this place and hung upon the tree until dead."

The incongruities of life on the trail are often surprising, especially to the modern mind. Who would have thought that the Sabbath would have affected the plans of people enduring such hardship? In spite of the seizures of piety referred to sardonically by Sharp in his entry for May 29, life on the trail was more often than not lawless and amoral, as witnessed by S. Miller, who was killed by Lafayette Sale. And yet, consider Sharp's entry for June 20, dutifully identified as Sunday:

> We came to Platte River after four miles. Five miles further on we crossed Big Deer Creek and encamped balance of day because it was Sunday. Some went hunting, some fishing, and others reset wagon tires by way of keeping the day. A number of trains rolled in this evening and camped along creek. There is good grass and clear running water. The stream is 20 feet wide and shaded with cottonwoods. A mail carrier came along today, 16 days from Kanesville, Iowa. he counted 3000 wagons between there and Fort Laramie. He says there is a great deal of sickness behind, as many as 13 dying out of one train. There were 1500 Mormon wagons crossing Missouri River when he left. We learned that Hon. Henry Clay died 20th of May. Mail carrier left two papers with us, dated 2nd of June. He expects to get to Salt Lake 30th of June, making the trip in 26 days. He travels with horse and buggy, and gets something to eat from emigrants.

1. Parkman, who'd crossed several years earlier, was more specific. He cited prices at Ft. Laramie as $2.00 for a cup of sugar; five cents worth of tobacco, $1.50; and bullets at seventy cents a pound. *The Journals of Francis Parkman*, (London, nd), vol. 2, p. 440.

BOOKING IN THE HEARTLAND

This is a quaint picture, to be sure: a mail carrier in his horse and buggy, ticking along the trail between wagon trains. And the thought of those 3,000 wagons encountered makes us feel almost claustrophobic, until we realized what an awful attenuation was required to extend them over so many miles. It is remarkable, when you stop to think about it, that they could find it so remarkable. And yet there were stretches where the trail was congested even by today's standards, and several times Sharp mentions that their party was never out of sight of other trains, ahead and before.

During the remainder of the diary, events are soberly recorded, including a relief from land robber prices. On August 19, Sharp mentions "some California bakeshops" where pies are sold at only seventy-five cents each and bread is available at forty cents a loaf. In Idaho, he encounters an Irishman who sells whiskey at twenty-five cents a drink.

The longest entry is that of August 22, a Sunday, appropriately, for Sharp's party is about to throw itself onto the great desert beyond Carson's Sink, Nevada.

> We started early this morning on to the desert. Here is a trading post and a government relief station. The desert is 48 miles across, sandy and barren, excepting for some greasewood that grows over it and one salt spring 12 miles from sink. Ten miles from spring we came to a trading post. All of these posts keep whiskey and water to sell. At this post I paid 25 cents for a quart of water. Near here we took supper and started on, I walking, as I had to do, for the man's team that was hauling my clothes was not able to haul me. We come to trading posts every two or three miles. We are never out of sight of lights. Traders ride back and forth at a run buying and giving out cattle. We arrived at Carson River (Nevada) this morning about sun-up, nearly given out, having walked 52 miles without stopping longer than to eat or drink. The last twelve miles was a deep, heavy sand. We are now in what is called Rag Town. Boarding houses, whiskey shops, hay yards and bakeries are about the extent of it. We here water our teams and move up the river five miles, which makes 56 miles on a stretch. I saw only three dead animals on the desert which had died this year, but hundreds lay here from 1850, dried up with skins over the bones. Hundreds of wagon frames lay on both sides of the road. At Rag Town we saw some hay yards corralled with wagon tires and log chains gathered from the desert.

This was the greatest trial of the westward journey in terms of simple physical hardship—women were sometimes so dehydrated that their skin never lost its wrinkles—but it is evident that much had been done to populate that arid stretch so that the miserable could at least have company.

Shortly after this entry, Robert Sharp ran out of paper and for the remainder of his account, his son William's epilogue must suffice. But his modest literary effort is enough to earn Sharp a place in William Coyle's *Ohio Authors and Their Books* (Cleveland, 1962), in which it is noted that in 1863 Sharp served in the Fairfield County militia, "a regiment which took an active part in pursuing and capturing the Morgan Raiders." After the war, Sharp settled down, quarrying stone and shipping it throughout the Midwest. By this time, of course, he and his childhood sweetheart had started a large family.

One of the things we keep forgetting about the Old West is that it was not populated by westerners at all, but by easterners. Before the Civil War, more frontiersmen came from Ohio than from any other state or territory. The reasons are obvious: Ohio was the first and most populous of the "western" (i.e., trans-Allegheny) states, and it had been settled by precisely the kind of people who go forth in search of adventure.

Sharp was one of these, even though he did not actually stay to settle in California. But then, the population beyond the Mississippi was nothing if not volatile; and three of the men Sharp met returning from California were from Circleville, Ohio . . . coming back home, whether wealthy or empty handed, Sharp does not say, but one tends to assume the latter.

Most of those who lived by their nerve and threw themselves into the great adventure of the plains and mountains beyond were a particular sort of people. Hardy and adventurous, of course; and few had reasons as valid and sober as Sharp's—but even these were not sufficient to keep Sharp himself from seriously contemplating his own return. In the last analysis, it seems to have been the terrible *bother* of turning back that kept him going.

As for all those who lived on their nerve and risked everything, one of the surprising facts about the Old West that seems utterly incompatible with our conventionalized notions is the high incidence of suicide.[2] But then, really, this should not be surprising at

2. So much is true and amply documented; however, there is one factor that weakens any attempt at statistical accuracy: there were times and places where

all. If you look closely at accounts such as that contained in Sharp's diary, you can see the terrible open-endedness of their life; it would require packaging in history, or in some small sample of history, such as a personal diary, to make sense and order out of those events.

Not everyone was able to do this; not everyone had Robert Lee Sharp's resources of character, his steadfastness and courage. But his account takes note of such people, and we can still feel the loss and terror of that young man and his wife, for example, who had been turned away from the wagon train by her own father: their dead child is a blind spot in their vision, even under the noonday sun; and no matter how relentlessly the wagons keep coming along the trail, they can feel the awful openness of the plains, with the wind blowing on them out of nowhere, and all that darkness and ignorance in all directions, and all of those bleached bones stacked like ruined churches alongside the trail.

---

murders were labeled suicides either for fear of evoking unpleasant consequences if prosecution were undertaken or simply to avoid the bother and expense of a criminal investigation . . . especially in those cases where the dignity and reputation of the corpse seemed hardly to justify so much extra work.

Words from Another Century

Once, at a country auction in Morgan County, Ohio, I purchased the first five of Marcius Willson's *Readers* designed for school children over a hundred years ago. These particular copies were remarkable because they were in pristine condition—unused, unread, and to all appearances, untouched by human (much less, schoolboy) hands. The characteristic survivals from schoolbooks of the mid-nineteenth century come to us in a battered and scarred condition. Usually the pages have been sliced and carved by quill pens, pencil shards, and catfish horns, and the cardboard covers are often morbidly bloated from dampness and mildew. But these particular copies were, as I mentioned, fresh, crisp, and new; and I was able to open them with something like the sensation with which countless children a century ago opened identical books at the beginning of a school term.

All of the expected outrages of our despised Victorian heritage are represented in these books. The "lessons" are precisely that—heavily moralistic parables and fables focused with deadly intent upon the minds of children, with no nonsense about "learning through doing" or "social adjustment." It is obvious that the ideas behind these books have to do with a child's learning, not through doing (disastrous risk!), but through listening and thus being instructed and edified by those (the author of the piece, the editor of the text, and the schoolmaster) who knew a great deal more about living than these children were likely soon to discover for themselves.

Rather than "social adjustment," the child was expected not to adjust to his callow and ignorant peers in a schoolroom that was to be regarded as a microcosm of society or the world, but was expected to adjust quickly and categorically to the dicta of text and master. It was, to express it in another way, a unilateral commitment; and there are still multitudes among us who feel that the unfairness to so many children resulted in endless heritable damage. It was in this nineteenth-century version of "adjustment" that the hated chore of memorization (often by rote) found its place; and with a little imagination you can still—in this enlightened day—hear the groans of the thick-witted, the obstinate, and those who might today be termed "independent" emanating from that benighted era. It is strange to think that such an incubus of pedagogy did not destroy every precious flower of morality and intellect that was struggling to come forth in that day, but the fact is that an uncomfortably large number of gifted people were to emerge from such schools as these and the similar schools of the previous generation. I guess it just proves . . . well, I'm not sure what.

If the moralistic tone of Marcius Willson's texts seems artless and woefully simplistic to the modern reader, in other ways the books are vastly more sophisticated in content than comparable texts today. The Third Reader, for instance, was used as early as the fourth grade, for students nine years old. Its first pages are devoted to "Elements of Elocution."[1] In this section I find such a sentence as the following: "The *monotone*, which is a succession of words on the same key or pitch, and is not properly an inflection, is often employed in passages of solemn denunication, sublime description, or expressing deep reverence and awe."

Subsequent sections of the book are "Stories from the Bible," "Moral Lessons," "Zoology," and miscellaneous writings. The vocabulary of the first two sections is somewhat relaxed, although such words as "lamentation," "bereaved," "unabated," "cupidity," and "benevolent" appear. Difficult words such as these are footnoted and defined, as they would have to be today for most readers of high school age.

In the Third Reader's chapters on zoology, the vocabulary and the conceptualization that the understanding of words entails are simply remarkable. Consider the section in "Mammalia" titled,

---

1. It should be noted, however, that the "grades" of the graded readers did not necessarily correspond to the "grades" of today's classes. Thus, the "Third Reader" was not confined to students in what we would today call "the third grade." It was simply undertaken after a student had mastered the second.

"Hoofed Quadrupeds (Ungulata). First Division: Thick-skinned quadrupeds; embracing the elephant, rhinoceros, hippopotamus, horse, swine, hyrax, tapir, etc." I like to think of the nine-, ten-, and eleven-year-old scholars "embracing" such elephantine, rhino-cerotic, and hyracid terms as Mr. Willson trotted before them: "verdure," "infusoria," "palmated," "annelidans," "karroo," "sward," and "ruminating."

If we are likely to be impressed by the vision of school children standing in recitation and sending forth learned sounds from their innocent throats, our admiration should be tempered by at least two considerations. The first is that (as the "progressivists"—if such are still to be found—would be the first to point out) the mere ability to repeat whole pages of orders, classes, and genera does not in itself indicate much of an understanding of the material. "Infusoria" and "karroo" can be as meaningless as "do, re, mi, fa, so" in those first lessons given for children to learn the names of the notes in the scale. Secondly, the information itself (in spite of the fancy nomenclature) is pretty elementary taxonomy in comparison to the vocabulary, if not in comparison to the ages of the learners.

Furthermore, in terms of modern science, a lot of the information is simply inaccurate. In Willson's Fourth Reader, the old business of the ostrich hiding its head when it becomes alarmed is included, albeit in a rather hesitant manner. In the above-mentioned material on thick-skinned quadrupeds, a picture of an elephant is given; and a very strange picture it is. Since it is the reproduction of a drawing, I suppose the work can be called inspired rather than merely accurate. At any rate, the head is recognizable; but the back is long and sloping, like that of a quarter horse, and the hindquarters are a stunning anomaly—thick and bellows-shaped, like the massively sagging pants of a pensive clown. A curious beast to be released into the jungles of an untutored mind.

In the last analysis, these are not overwhelmingly important objections, when one considers the purpose of the book. Words are remembered best when they make sense—when they are understood—and I for one like the idea of ten-year-olds uttering the words "ruminating" and "palmated." To be sure, the utterance alone is not enough, but in the learning of *any* discipline, a vocabulary is simply indispensable. The words are never anything less than the first great stride toward understanding a science or a field of scholarship. And as for the inaccuracies, these are of two kinds—those of oversimplification and those of error. The first is always necessary for the instruction of children in complicated matters, and the second is obviously and easily remediable.

For the really striking quality of Marcius Willson's old-fashioned book, however, one must turn from such things as the advanced vocabulary and the high demands upon factual knowledge made of these children and come back to the moralistic character of the book. Here is where the modern reader will face something which appears at once very strange and very familiar. The hypocrisies of the Victorian era seem still to be with us, but in reality they are not. They have been replaced by other hypocrisies.

There is one passage in Marcius Willson's book which he himself apparently wrote, since it is ascribed to no other writer. Regardless of its authorship, it affords quite simply—for all its artlessness— some very good reading. This section is titled, "Three Lessons of Industry," and beneath the title there are three pictures, side-by-side, showing an oak tree, a small boy studying at his desk and a coral reef. Underneath these pictures is written

> 1. How very small is the little plant that springs up from the acorn, and how slowly it grows! and yet, by growing a little each day, and year by year, it finally becomes a mighty oak; and the birds sing in its branches, and many cattle repose in its shade.

> 2. There are little coral insects that begin to work away down on the bottom of the ocean: they build there cell after cell, one upon another, like little grains of sand. But day by day, and year by year, these little insects keep cheerfully toiling on, never stopping to rest or to play, until, at length, their rocky dwellings reach above the water; and in this way beautiful islands are formed, and men go and dwell on them.

> 3. "Little by little, and lesson after lesson, I will gather up the knowledge which I find in books, and in the world around me," said a thoughtful boy. And by learning a little every day, and learning it well, he became, at length, a wise and useful man, honored and respected by all who knew him.

I don't know whether you paused, as I did, at that part about the little insects toiling "cheerfully." That is a bit excessive, to be sure. But the first passage, particularly, has for me some of the simple beauty of the Psalms in the King James version. And when I read that this young scholar grew into a "wise and useful man," I am ready to sign almost anything.

But what is it to be wise and useful? From the context in which this phrase appears, it is evident that these words both refer to moral, cultural qualities, for it is said of our hypothetical young scholar that he was "honored and respected by all who knew him." And, though we must allow a certain diversity of views concerning them, these words do not come flying to us out of the darkness, but carry with them echoes and associations. Wisdom, for instance, does not reflect mere knowledge or expertise, but a richly human understanding. It is a moral as well as an intellectual habitude. It is an environment of heart and mind, a versatility in adjustment wedded to a consistency of character or principle. It is, above all, an ability to cope with life and to govern oneself. Wisdom happens only after the accumulation of experience and the weathering of good and bad seasons. It is the result, as well as the manifestation, of many things—a clear head, a healthy acceptance of life, the courage to be responsible for what one does, a sense of the reality of others, and—let us not forget—industry.

Where does wisdom end, according to the above definitions, and usefulness begin? Clearly, the two qualities blend together, and I'm not so sure that the question needs answering with anything that sounds like certitude. The Victorians did not lack self-confidence, and their definitions of "wise" and "useful" would surely sound smug and self-righteous to our troubled ears.

But there is importance simply in the fact—not that the children of the 1860s were given satisfactory definitions of wisdom and usefulness—but that they were given such words, along with countless examples of wise and useful acts, showing what it was believed men should and could be. If these children grew up in educational strait jackets, and if they marched through their early years in some kind of lock step, they nevertheless learned very early that wisdom and usefulness were very great and abiding ideals of human conduct. No matter how much corruption, ignorance, and sloth he found in the life around him, or in himself, a graduate of the nineteenth-century American elementary readers had a notion of what these things were—knew what to call them and knew they were meant to be despised.

After studying these old readers, I decided to look at some modern fourth grade textbooks, and here again I was surprised. One of the differences I had anticipated was in the matter of "heroes." I had heard and read that modern textbooks extolled the average man and child presumably in the service of helping most people adjust well to the facts of their lives, since, by definition, most people have only mediocre talents and intelligence. But in the books I consulted, this wasn't entirely true. Although the majority of the stories might indeed have glorified the average in human behavior, there were nevertheless stories about heroes. In one modern fourth grade textbook, for example, I found stories about Washington, Lincoln, Benjamin Franklin, the Wright brothers, and Annie Oakley. There were also fictional tales about "The Amiable Giant," "Paul Bunyan," "Chanticleer," and "The Ugly Duckling," along with stories from Aesop and *Alice in Wonderland.*

By contrast, the heroes in the nineteenth-century readers were mostly biblical—Moses, David, Elijah, and Jesus. Lincoln, of course, was not a likely inclusion, and the Wright brothers were even less likely.

In some respects, the modern reader is as moralistic as the older one. While the old book inculcates with a directness that sometimes abuses good sense, the modern book tends to sugar-coat the most tepid truisms of good will and tolerance. A group of children are pictured playing on a city sidewalk. One of them is unquestionably black, though somewhat bleached and depersonalized, just as the white children are. They all, in fact, look a little like fixtures in the window of a clothing store.[2]

One might not expect to find the racial theme in one of Willson's books, but in the Second Reader, an unidentified "Miss Mary" goes to the kitchen to instruct "Susan" in the baking of pies. There is a picture of the scene, and in the text following the picture, one finds the question, "Is Susan a white woman?" Clearly, she is not. A few lines further down, the following passage appears: "What has Susan on her head? Are her arms as white as Miss Mary's? Is her face as white? Are her hands black? Yes, but they are as clean as they would be if they were white."

In all fairness, it must be said that the modern readers are unquestionably happier. Obviously books that are separated by a span of a hundred years cannot be compared too closely in either content

---

2. This was written in the late 1960s. Almost twenty years later, today's elementary texts are different in their concern for and sensitivity toward ethnic and racial representation. Their artwork is brilliant in all senses of that word; and from the sampling I've seen, I am tempted to believe that today's readers are more sophisticated, and show a greater respect for excellence, than those of the sixties.

or approach. Still, they are somewhat comparable in terms of rationale and principle. And it is in such perspectives that texts of today reveal something quite extraordinary.

I mentioned that today's books are "unquestionably happier," and it is indeed this sunny quality that impresses a reader after he turns from the grim parables of a Willson Reader. Our modern books are filled with bright, colored pictures showing cheery children *having fun*. If they are learning something, very good (and beyond doubt, much can be learned from these books), but the obvious thing about the pictures and the stories is the good times these kiddies are having. It has to be this way—one hears the writers and editors of such books saying—because school books have to compete with TV, plastic toys, video games, moving pictures, candy, and other sweets in unheard-of quantities. And they are right. Just like their parents, modern American children are in the seemingly enviable position of having vast numbers of people knocking themselves out trying to get them to have fun—to enjoy themselves a little more—to cultivate new forms of entertainment and pleasure.

It is scarcely surprising, then, that the modern school books I looked at did not hint at the fact that life is anything but sunny afternoons, indulgent parents, policemen, balloon men, zoo attendants, bus drivers in a world filled with amity and concern for others . . . a world where kindness and hospitality are no less dependable than the laws of gravity. The stories are exclusively about good guys, and one wonders how a nine-year-old child can reconcile the adventures he reads about in school with the dirty-faced kid next door, the cheater-at-marbles, or the bus driver who is fed up with kids and loses his temper.

In this regard, Marcius Willson's old books are dramatically different. In the Second Reader, there are stories about "an Angry Man" and "a Railroad Thief," both of whom, you may be sure, get their comeuppance. The Railroad Thief's name is Tobin—which intrigues me, for some reason; but the real villain of the Second Reader is a fellow with the marvelous name of "Lazy Slokins." This villain is the protagonist of a number of episodes that constitute what is almost a full biography of wickedness and sloth. He is shown first as a lazy schoolboy who mutilates and neglects his books (according to the evidence, there must have been many Slokins in those days). Then Slokins appears as an even lazier young man, who, in the midst of the narrative, elicits this exasperated and quaintly worded aside: "Why don't he get up and go to work?"

Eventually, Slokins becomes a drunkard and finally a thief, after which appears "The Robin's Temperance Song."

A hundred years have turned Slokins into a colorful sort of rogue, and neither the illustrations of his epic story nor the bilious suggestiveness of his name help the matter. Still, in the context of the times, this was deadly serious business. Anyone who knows the history of nineteenth-century America understands that drunkenness was, indeed, an appalling problem, and one doesn't have to be an abstainer to think so.

But this, of course, is another matter. The importance here is the fact that the miserable history of Slokins was told, moralized upon, and footnoted in these pages. It is possible that such stories as this only helped teach vindictiveness and moral snobbery to the young of a genus that needs no training in such skills. But it is also possible that children reading about liars, thieves, and drunkards were nourished and edified to realize that the world of books was, after all, concerned with *all* of the life around them.

It was in such a context that they were meant to see Slokins, who had *not* grown into "a wise and useful man, honored and respected by all who knew him." And as they could believe in the reality of Slokins, whose kind was present in villages and cities throughout the land, so they could believe in the reality of those ideals by which the man's failure was measured. They were sturdy and inspiring ideals, and they must be seen against a background of "reality." We still have need for such yardsticks, for Slokins still abides with us, even though he might not smell of rum or wear a slouch hat and dress in nineteenth-century breeches. He still abides with us, but he is not represented in the textbooks our children read. One has to go back a hundred years to the sort of schoolbook Marcius Willson made for that sort of realism.

In my chronic search for old and rare books, I am often subject to misconceptions of what constitutes rarity in a book. The most frequent misconception is that McGuffey Readers are instrinsically, and without exception, rare.

Willson's Readers and McGuffey's are remarkably alike, the chief difference being the relative scarcity of the former. McGuffey's are everywhere, however; they were printed by the millions, and in all my years of collecting and searching out rare books, I have come upon only two copies that are theoretically rare: one, the Eclectic Fourth Reader's first edition, published in Cincinnati in

1837. This was in leather, missing part of the spine; and I traded it sometime in the 1960s, at a valuation of $15.

And yet, I have seen dirty, badly chewed, water-stained late reprints sell at a country auction for ten and fifteen dollars. In the context of such auctions, that is what these books were worth; the only thing is, they were bought out of ignorance, and you can't depend upon having two such ignorant bidders present when you decide to sell your books.

Behind all this grumbling lies a message of hope. Like the Willson's, those McGuffey readers are worth having. They are, in a word, "collectible." Not because they will likely appreciate in value—I doubt that they will in the near future, unless you can find those two bidders I spoke of at the same auction—they might not have learned this lesson yet (a lesson that the readers in question never take up). Nevertheless, these old readers are important and highly significant testaments concerning America in the nineteenth century and its existential struggle to create itself.

I am tempted to argue that every Americana collection should have a few copies of them, complete with old woodcuts or later illustrations, to document how our ancestors once tried to raise their children and thereby create the next generation (our great- and great-great-grandparents) according to ideals shared by virtually everyone.

The best part of this sort of collecting is, it's cheap. You won't need to spend more than the cost of a meal for two in a good restaurant. If you are patient, that is, and are willing to bide your time and wait for copies in decent condition. This last is the hardest part, because those books were generally read to pieces. That's part of what makes them so worth having.

Charley Smith's River

Old manuscript diaries possess a unique charm, simply and naturally, because of what they are. So far as I know, graphology as a means for character analysis has no real claim to credibility. And yet, like fingerprints, handwriting is exclusive to the individual, and at any specific time (a necessary qualification since our handwriting changes) there are exactly as many handwritings in the world as there are literate people. This fact belongs to the class of symbols, which means it is a fact that suggests a larger, less factual reality, even though, as is the way with symbols, there is no way to say exactly what this larger reality is.

Nevertheless, it can be felt. And this feeling is itself the unique charm mentioned above. In a diary (or journal—not quite the same thing) one is able to see the almost literal traces of a person's thoughts, day by day, focused by word and configuration as only that person could focus them. But within this realm of generic charm, there is naturally a great range, extending all the way from "A clear mild day, went to see Cousin Sally" to accounts of extraordinary happenings and/or profound contemplations. The difference is the presence of mind—which doesn't say anything negative about the diarist: only that a genius can be dull in a diary, but a dullard cannot be interesting.

And yet, even the most prosaic of entries is possessed of the simple majesty of recorded fact. When sixteen-year-old Charles Allen Smith, from Pomeroy, Ohio, signed on the *Kate Timmons* as a deck hand in 1885, he was ill prepared to rhapsodize over the "beauteous sights afforded by Nature," as the high style of the times required. Instead, when confronted by the ineffable, as on his first visit to New Orleans (on December 18, with the weather warm and clear), he states simply: "The City is a fine one, it beats all my expectation. I cannot describe it, I spent almost a day in the City, came to the boat tired slept all night."

Probably most readers would prefer a style not quite so laconic; we wish Charley Smith (he had to be "Charley") had given a shot at describing the city, and it might be interesting to have more details about what he did that day and maybe know why he was so tired. Sustained excitement inspired by the exotic surroundings and constant walking could tire out anybody, even a sixteen-year-old boy; but it would nevertheless be good to know exactly what happened to Charley—what he saw and what he did and, maybe, what was done to him that day. Evidently nothing too dramatic, or it probably would have gotten into his diary. Unless it was *too* dramatic, in the sense of *too much;* in which case, Charley—like a good Victorian youth—would have kept quiet about the whole business and not written a word. After all, his mother and father might be reading these entries. Or his sisters. Or future wife and children.

Which brings up the question, To whom is a diary addressed? All speech is transactional, by necessity, and is therefore addressed to someone, either actually, as in a letter, or implicitly, as in . . . well, a diary. When Pepys and William Byrd encoded their diaries, they were merely emphasizing the privacy of the genre, in contrast to journals, which record daily events just as relentlessly, but with significantly different focus and intent. Journals are meant to serve some sort of public or professional occasion.

Most diaries are, of course, addressed to oneself. And anyone who has kept one for any period of time will have experienced the amazement common to all diarists at how much we naturally forget—how much would have been forgotten if events of each day had not been faithfully transcribed. When old men keep diaries (or old women, though historically this is less evident), it is often for the sake of posterity, and they are therefore vitiated or altered (depending upon many factors, of course) by a sense of audience, effect, and the strategic impurities of rhetoric.

But there is an innocence in manuscript diaries kept by the young and never published. When Charley Smith left Racine, Ohio, on the *Kate Timmons,* he had an idea of what a glorious adventure awaited him. Travel in those days was not common, easy, or cheap—a trip to Chillicothe was something of an event, but New Orleans! A tropical city that was foreign in more ways than one.

This was in November, 1885, the year that *Huckleberry Finn* was published, and when he signed on as deck hand, Charley was only two years older than the immortal Huck. The great Mississippi River that Twain wrote about most lyrically was not that of 1885, but the one remembered from his youth; and yet, the river had not changed much in those thirty or forty years. Charley Smith, in his entry of November 27, wrote:

> Still at the bank, left here at 2 o'clock in the afternoon passing a very rough lot of country also passing the Caven rock at half past four in the afternoon. This Caven rock is the great robers den occupied by robers in years passed. It is on the Illanois shore at the foot of a great ledge of limestone about a mile long and 150 feet high and there is but one way to get to it that is from the lower end.

This reference is to the Ohio River and to the legends of Mike Fink, but Twain would have known the scene intimately, as would Tom and Huck.

The shores were mostly unrelieved forest. Charley mentions how little settled the country bordering the river was immediately south of Cairo (which he consistently spells "Cario"). In his November 29 entry, he states:

> The afternoon was spent in running on a big and smooth river, passing a wild and desolate country covered with dense forest of cotton wood. Winding up the business of the day by being on watch from half past 9 in the morning until 6 in the evening, went to the bank at half past five o'clock in the evening after supper a lot of us went out and took a ramble through the woods finding nothing but brush, came back and went to bed, slept all night, made 80 miles Monday morning.

Two details in this entry are of interest. The first is Charley's use of the indefinite article "a" in referring to what is, after all, the same river they have been traveling on and will continue to travel on until they reach its mouth. This implies that the river is different things at different times: the same river, referred to as "a" river in one context ("big and smooth") can and will become another river in another context. Also, the entry states (as do others) that the *Kate Timmons* did not always run at night, but where the channel was dangerous or unfamiliar moored, nosed into the bank.

Even at that relatively late date, steamboat travel was chancy enough without taking the risk of feeling for the channel after dark, where it was known to be tricky. There are several references to skeletons of old boats: "Saw the sunken steamer Schreaves Port a totle reck," the entry for December 5 states. And two days before, Charley wrote:

> Pulled out at day break from Memphis, weather clear and cold, the forenoon past without any trouble, passing a sunken barge belonging to the Mississippi Valey transptation Co. loaded with 25000 bushel of corn in the bulk and 1200 bails of cotton, the day turned out fair and warm, made a good run passing over some rough river pulled in for the night at a cotton farm in Arkansas, making a run of sixty miles today. Slept all night, pulled out at day light.

But there were stretches of river that were more familiar to the captain or known to be safe with wide channels. One such place was immediately south of Baton Rouge, which the *Kate Timmons* passed on December 15, and the name of which Charley spells in his own sturdily independent way:

> Here at Baton Rushe we saw the first oranges growing, they looked beautiful green and ripe one growing on the same tree. We sold 120 barrels of apples at $2.00 a bl. Left Baton Rushe at 12 o'clock being a fine afternoon warm and sunny, I saw in Baton Rushe the Penetenshrey, they work their men on public works about 4 miles below town, I saw about 100 men working on the levey. It is a fine country down here, sugar plantations on both sides of the river and every plantation has a sugar mill on it. It is nice to see the beautiful groves of live oak trees in front of some Residence. There was Stirn Wheel Steam boat passed us this afternoon loaded with cotton, 15 teers across her head, 9 teers deep, and 3 teers wide, on the gards out side of her calbon, she was a monstor. Still the country improves, we run all night.

Naturally, there were adventures along the way, some calculated and some not. The former were connected with excursions ashore, such as when they laid over at Helling, Arkansas:

> After eating dinner, we took a strole in town, was gone an hour and a half when they took a notion to leave, blew the whistle for us, but we were out so far, and saw so much it made us late in reaching the boat, the Captain grew impatient, started out leaving a yawl on shore for us to follow. Out in town we saw lots of darkies and a great many beautiful residences. Left the bank at half past two, saw the St. Francis River, a beautiful stream in Arkansas large enough for small steamers. It looks stranger down here at this time of year and see the willows green. Went to bank at five o'clock laid at the first goverment light below Freighers Point in Tennessee. At six o'clock the same evening the wind commenced to blow and the longer the worse it

blew until we thought that every thing would go to peaces it lasted until late in the night. Stood our regular watch. made 20 miles.

There were also excursions ashore to pick nuts and hunt game to add variety to their menu. Charley mentions rabbits, coon, squirrel, and even an owl. He doesn't say whether they ate the owl or not, but the other game must have been a welcome enrichment of their diet, if what the cook of the *Kate Timmons* served on Christmas day is any indication. Charley states that they had "a fine Christmas breakfast, fried potatoes, without salt, cold turnips, strong butter, black coffee, and Oh what bread, and fat meat and hard tack."

One can see from this that Charley was no gourmet; not only that, his culinary standards were modest—a fact of considerable importance in view of his comments on the rest of the fare for that day: "Christmas dinner potatoes with the skins on, beans boilt with pork, bread hard tack, oysters boiled in Mississippi sandy water and some fried." Bad enough by anyone's standards; but Charley ends this sad entry with the laconic statement: "Supper still worse, run all night being no fog."

As for the unplanned adventures, they had to do with more-or-less predictable mishaps in river travel at that time. One of these happened early, on the morning of November 30, while they were still on the Ohio:

Left the bank at half past five, the country showing more farming land, the banks being higher and the land better. Finding a crack in long Cylender timber, run until five o'clock in the evening, got in the steamer Frisbey swells and almost shipwrecked us. We were trying to land made a terrible rough landing, one produce boat took an old tree root, the coal boats taking the land breaking all of that side of the fleet loose, it was fun to see the Captain, he tried to be all over the boat in a minute. Some times with a line on his shoulder then again saying get a tow-line. He ran upstairs for a line, grabed the line, struck his head against a stanchen, nocked him backwards, gathered his line and lit out made all safe laid all night.

Well, we all know about the loneliness of command, but this is surely a new variation.

Then there was the confrontation on New Year's Day, 1886:

We met a little coaster and he thought that the Pilot was going to run over him so he got his pistol and said he would shoot if he did not hold her out so Billy stoped the engines and ran for his revolver then the man began to roe and Billy began to shoot. It was fun, the woman was swearing out of a window and the first shot she closed the window and that was the last we saw of her, they roed for life, when he knew he was out of reach of the revolver he fired one shot with his horse pistol. At three o'clock this morning it commenced to rain.

One of the glories of such unlettered prose is the jamming of time into unlikely cartons of syntax. There is also the supposition, on the part of the truly ignorant, that the reader is in possession of facts that he could have no way of knowing. But of course, this is a diary, and Charley wasn't really obligated to any reader but himself.

Nevertheless, the effect is often hilarious beyond the hilarity Charley Smith himself obviously found in this anecdote. No doubt it was "fun" to exchange some handgun fire with a smaller boat, but where did that woman come from? She hadn't even been mentioned. She sticks her head into the account just long enough to pull it back and slam the hatch after her.

There's a story in that, and we are reminded that every good story carries a cargo of untold stories with it, all of that which is suggested and left untold, all of that which might be seen as implicit in that which is stated.

I bought Charles Allen Smith's diary from a man near Pomeroy several years ago. He lived out in the country and had a late Victorian book of illustrations, a squat and ugly little quarto, which he offered to me for $30 and which I declined.

"But I know I can get that for this book at a flea market," he said, tapping it with his index finger.

"That's fine," I told him. "Go ahead. I couldn't get any more than that for it myself, so if you can sell it for thirty dollars, fine."

He nodded and then when I asked about some miscellaneous volumes nearby, he shrugged and offered them all to me for ten dollars. I looked at them briefly and accepted his offer.

Charley Smith's diary was part of this assortment. It doesn't look like much. Your first instinct is to throw it away, and that instinct is often a healthy one. The diary doesn't exactly *look* like a diary; it is written in pencil on a small lined tablet—the sort that was used in schools then in the late nineteenth century, and was so used until a few years ago. No doubt Charley was comfortable writing in such a tablet, for the evidence suggests that he didn't go beyond the fifth or sixth grade, and he probably needed straight horizontal lines to keep his handwriting under control. I myself can remember such a time when I was in the early grades of school, wondering how people managed to write straight without those pale-blue lines to guide them.

Needless to say, however, I value Charley Smith's tablet diary far more than any Victorian picture book I have ever seen. In spite of what they might bring at a flea market. In his own way, Charley is an artist, too, and the fact that he is a primitive and therefore unconventionalized is precisely what makes his own "book" a particularly fascinating one, and rare to the point of uniqueness.

I've tried to find some references to Charley Smith in my Meigs County histories, wondering if he ever achieved enough prominence to be mentioned, but there is nothing. He would have been too young to be referred to by Stillman C. Larkin in *The Pioneer History of Meigs County,* which was published in 1908 by Larkin's nephew, but which was probably written about the time Charley Smith went to New Orleans. Edgar Ervin's later *Pioneer History of Meigs County* (np, 1949) does not mention Charley, but Ervin does refer to a "Captain George Smith, a well-known steamboat captain and boat owner who owned some thirteen steamboats during his boating career"; and then Ervin adds, "He died some years ago at Racine, Ohio."

Well, such is fame. To think that this is practically all we know about Captain George, along with the fact that he was one of nine children of John and Elizabeth Smith, who'd emigrated there from Weston, (West) Virginia. Perhaps the boy who wrote about his river trip was a nephew or son of George. Racine was and is small enough that there can't be too many people by the name of Smith, even, who aren't related.

But in a way it's appropriate that Charles Smith didn't live to become a state senator or a colonel in the Spanish-American War. Maybe he died of pneumonia or was burned alive in a gambling house fire near the end of the century. Maybe anything.

All we know is, he saw Memphis from the river and got all the way to New Orleans, and the trip there and back was enough to inspire him to sit down with his pencil and write down his daily record of the major events of that fabulous journey. And now, beyond any doubt, more people have heard about him and have even read part of what he wrote about his trip than such a fellow would have dreamed possible.

Books and Learning on the Frontier,
God Help Us

In 1803, when the citizens of Ames Township in Athens County, Ohio, gathered to deliberate upon the needs of that raw frontier community, the first subject taken up was road improvement, and the second was intellectual fulfillment. This second concern resulted in the famous "Coonskin Library"—later given that name because the books were financed through the sale of furs—the first public library in the Northwest Territory.

The reason for such a high priority given to books is obvious, in a way: these people were isolated in a wilderness, and they craved the printed word, which connected them not only with the country at large but civilization itself. The only newspaper they read was *The American Gazette,* which arrived approximately once every three months. But the news they craved was not confined to the happenings of the day; rather, it was news in the larger sense— information about the greater world of the Past, history, and information about the adventures of the mind and human spirit. They wanted works of the imagination as well as fact; and by 1830 a forty-four-volume set of the Waverly novels was part of the library—conveying news of Scott's timeless epic imagination rather than of the latest enthusiasms from Congress or the White House.

The books of this early library were guarded jealously: thumb, grease, and burn marks brought a fine strictly determined according to the size; and overdue books always cost the borrower, in spite of the frequent hardships of fording flooded streams or plodding through snow banks to return them. But the books circulated vigorously. In 1826, 462 books were borrowed (a great number for so small a population), and one man, Daniel Weethee, accounted for thirty-six of these himself.

The Coonskin Library was an inspiring example for a frontier community, but it did not signal an unqualified dedication to books and learning. Frontier schools in southeastern Ohio were, like other frontier schools throughout the Midwest, a chancy and uneven enterprise. In fact, many sizable communities had no schools of any sort, and a child might learn to read almost by accident, if at all. In 1837, Samuel Lewis reported that there were still Ohio villages of 500 to 600 inhabitants without schools.

And where there were schools, not all was sweetness and light. Teachers were often qualified only negatively, in the sense that they were too old or otherwise incapacitated for more strenuous work, and since they might as well do something, they might as well teach school. Especially if they could read and add and subtract. As elsewhere in early nineteenth-century mid-America, alcohol was a problem, and the figure of the drunken schoolmaster was depressingly familiar. Some even placated their older and more rebellious students by making their whiskey or brandy jug available to them. This is not consistent with what is usually meant by the spirit of learning.

School buildings were seldom built as such; often they were simply cabins that had been abandoned by a family that had moved on to something better. Athens was an exception in this, for a school house was built on the Higgins property in 1801—the first in the county; and its first schoolmaster was a Massachusetts man named Bartlett.

Commonly, however, early schoolhouses were architectural hand-me-downs, and naturally somewhat humble. Long before he became president of Ohio University, William Holmes McGuffey taught briefly in an abandoned smoke house in Paris, Kentucky. Even if a schoolhouse was specially constructed, there was no guarantee that the results would be impressive. An early schoolhouse was built near Zanesville over a tree stump, which later served as the dunce's stool. The "floor" was clay, of course; so the dunce for the day might have been the most comfortable person present.

Students were usually required to supply their own textbooks, and there was one Athens County student who claimed to have actually learned to read solely from a treatise on predestination. Usually, especially in the higher grades, students stood up and recited their lessons in concert, singing out the passages from Franklin's *Autobiography* or Gray's *Elegy in a Country Churchyard,* as edited for the popular readers of the day.

Not all schoolmasters were unfit. Some were demanding and relatively sophisticated—especially those from New England (in contrast to the Scotch-Irish from the mountains of Virginia). Many of these would advertise in the local newspapers, reporting that they were setting up school and needed "scholars." Often they were paid in bizarre ways, with (as a Kentucky schoolmaster reported) "bear bacon, buffalo steak, jerked venison, furs, potmetal, bar iron, linsey, hackled flax, young cattle, pork, corn, or whiskey, as well as tobacco,"[1] as acceptable currency in the way of salary. This wasn't as bad as it might sound, if you consider the fiscal confusion of those days when there were dozens of banks in Ohio, issuing their own currencies independently, some of which had no more backing than the paper they were printed on.

The schools were only part of the cultural growth of that period, and from the evidence cited above, one can see this is fortunate. Many people on the frontier (not those who formed the Coonskin Library, however) or in the following generation believed that an ability to read at a primitive level and do simple arithmetic was all that the good life required. But, given even this elementary preparation, there were other ways for a young person to become educated. There were churches and debating societies here and there, which were generally supportive of and conducive to education; and for young men, there were printing shops, which involved constant reading, along with attention to language and form, and these provided some sort of equivalent to a college education for some of America's most renowned writers and statesmen.

Gradually, too, as individuals acquired property and wealth, they began to buy books for their private libraries, as the flourishing of booksellers in Philadelphia and elsewhere testifies. The most famous Philadelphia bookseller was Mathew Carey, many of whose books made their way by wagon and pack train across the mountains to Pittsburgh and from there down the river in flatboats and steamboats. Carey's most famous book agent was Parson Mason Weems, who became the Grandfather of Our Country, insofar as he created the myth of Washington in his famous biography—inventing the story of the cherry tree along with that of the cabbage seeds, as well as numerous other enthusiasms, most of which did not, like

1. See Epilogue.

that of the cherry tree, find their way into the McGuffey Readers or their counterparts.

It was at this time, too, that Cincinnati (coincidentally named for Washington, the "Cincinnatus of the West") became the major city beyond the mountains, as well as a thriving publishing center. Cincinnati's influence on American literature and thought was enormous at that time, and it helped shift the emphasis in reading from English to American authors. (In 1820, well over half the books read by Americans were either English books, as such, or books by English authors.)

Many of the books read by early Ohioans were of a somber religious character, and some parents discouraged the reading of novels as being either sinful or frivolous or both. The dime novels that appeared after the Civil War had no real equivalent at that earlier time, however, and the most deafening parental outcries were still two generations in the future.

As more people in the backwoods regions learned to read, newspapers as well as books began to circulate; and of course their role in the education of the people was constant and pervasive.

Among the most interesting cultural influences in early Ohio were the law courts, which provided entertainment and education for a populace badly in need of both. Most of us today live within a legal system devised by men who learned their law—not to mention oratory and dialectic—from the law courts of the early 1800s. In the first years there were no court houses as such, so court was held in a tavern or saloon or church or any other public building that was available. Judges and lawyers would travel their circuits, often riding on horseback together and debating old issues to pass the time. They stayed together in the same taverns at night, and for entertainment one would read aloud to the others—usually from a legal text or something equally edifying.

Here is the traveling court in those days, as described in B. A. Hinsdale's *Old Northwest:*

> The judges spent about as much time in the saddle as on the bench. Court and bar travelled through the wilderness, five or six together, sometimes seven or eight days on a single journey with a pack-horse to transport the supplies that they could not carry on their own horses or purchase by the way. When purchasing a horse, one of the first questions was whether he was a good swimmer. But that was the day when the mail was a week coming and going between Marietta and Zanesville; when the Post-General sometimes filled up mail schedules

and contracts with his own hand; and when the principal means of transportation on the Ohio was "the Ark," invented by one Krudger on the Juniata River—a square, flat-bottomed vessel, 40 ft in length by 15 in breadth, 6 ft deep, covered with a roof of thin boards, accommodated with a fireplace & carrying from 200 to 400 barrels of flour.[2]

An important part of Lincoln's education was derived from his experience with similar courts in Illinois, for they were a tough school for a young attorney. Flaws in logic or argumentation were closely regarded, and a man could be instantaneously converted into a hero or laughing stock, according to how he behaved himself in court, no matter how noble or trivial the cause.

That causes could be mightily trivial is evident in the case of Ferguson vs. Kelso, wherein the judge (with the marvelous name of Bowling Green—he was a friend of the young Lincoln) listened impatiently to the testimony in the case—which had to do with the ownership of a hog—and suddenly brought due process to an end, "declaring that the Plaintiff's witnesses were damned liars, the court being acquainted with the shoat in question and knowing it to belong to Jack Kelso."[3]

Like the early schoolteachers, lawyers in that day were unevenly qualified, which is a polite way of saying that some of them were scarcely qualified at all. But then the court officials themselves—and just about every other sort of official, too—were of various levels of professional training and inspiration. A man in Indiana ran for clerk of court on the platform that he'd "been sued on every section of the statute" and that he was, therefore, very familiar with the law.[4]

Lack of proper legal training, however, was not always a great detriment and seldom an inhibition. A young man of ambition gravitated naturally to the law, for he would naturally observe that it was the lawyers, above all others, who made the laws and (not always accidentally) often got rich. Furthermore, they were at the heart and center of one of the frontier's two major entertainment industries.

The other was afforded by religious camp meetings, which also provided entertainment of a sort, even though much of it was hysterical and ended in visions of eternal hellfire.

2. Hinsdale, B. A., *The Old Northwest* (New York, 1891), p. 303.
3. Woldman, Albert A., *Lawyer Lincoln* (Boston, 1936), p. 21.
4. Ibid., p. 18.

The excitement and popularity of such meetings were extraordinary, however. Mostly, camp meetings were sponsored by Presbyterians, Methodists, and Baptists, and when the message would "take" with a person (a little like small pox vaccine in its description), he or she would be "struck down" and carried out of the congregation. At one memorable meeting in Bourbon County, Kentucky, over 1,000 persons bit the dust. Perhaps a world record for that time.

In comparison with camp meetings, the entertainment provided by the law courts was downright sunny, even if a particular trial happened to eventuate in a man being sentenced to be hanged. This was still better than a wholesale consignment to hellfire; and if the sentence was a mere thirty days in jail, it might almost be considered a modest price to pay for providing so much colorful legal debate and oratory.

High rhetoric was very much approved of in those days, in spite of the raw and primitive life (or perhaps because of it) that people were forced to endure. If a lawyer could quote Latin, no matter how badly or incorrectly, the galleries would nod with approval between easing gobs of tobacco juice onto the puncheon floor or their neighbors' boots. And if a lawyer could make a witness cry— or better yet, the judge and jury—why, his fame was assured.

Nothing was deemed essentially ludicrous, if a lawyer could bring it off. Consider the following opening:

> May it please the Court and gentlemen of the jury—while Europe is bathed in blood, while classic Greece is struggling for her rights and liberties, and trampling the unhallowed altars of the bearded infidels to dust, while the chosen few of degenerate Italy are waving their burnished swords in the sunlight of liberty, while America shines forth the brightest orb in the political sky—I, I, with due diffidence, rise to defend the cause of this humble hog thief.[5]

Obviously, hog thefts—and the defense against charges thereof— were common in those days; one of the early names of Cincinnati was "Pork-opolis," indicative of the enormous importance of the hog market. (Maybe there is some dignity in the fact that the hog is the most intelligent animal in the barnyard, but such a fact doesn't totally eliminate the bathos in such arguments as that quoted.)

The authority of the courts was very shaky in those days, especially in the outlying regions. Sometimes the judge and his court

5. See Epilogue.

were lucky to escape from a town in one piece; sometimes they didn't. Often there was an insidious threat of retribution, and sometimes this was quite explicit, as in the following summary before a jury by a defense attorney:

> The law expressly declares, gentlemen, in the beautiful language of Shakespeare, that where a doubt of the prisoner exists, it is your duty to fetch him innocent. If you keep this fact in view, in the case of my client, gentlemen, you will have the honour of making a friend of him and all his relations, and you can allus look upon this occasion and reflect with pleasure that you have done as you would be done by. But, if, on the other hand, you disregard the principles of law and bring him in guilty, the silent twitches of conscience will follow you all over every fair cornfield, I reckon, and my injured and downtrodden client will be apt to light on you one of these nights as my cat lights on a saucerful of new milk.[6]

But the local champion of oratory was probably a man named Andrew Coffinberry, who argued (and no doubted chanted and roared) at the bar in the upper Hocking Valley from 1807 to 1836. Because of his addiction, not just to poetry, but to the writing and composing of same, he was known as the "Poet-Lawyer." He was also known as "Count Coffinberry," because of his eloquence in the court room.

Most of Count Coffinberry's oratory has washed down the drain of history, as has most of the oratory of his peers. But Coffinberry's case is unique, in that he wrote an epic poem, titled *The Forest Rangers,* which by some extraordinary fate was published in Columbus in 1842. It is difficult for the unbiased reader to believe that verse this bad could ever have been published without the author, or someone similarly benighted, subsidizing it. But published it was, and here is a passage from it, describing a fair maiden, captive of Indians, with almost every cliché in sight:

The nymph was beautiful as light,
Her skin was almost alabaster white,
Save, to her cheeks was lent
The damask rose's richest tint,
Her lips when parted did disclose,
Two fair and perfect pearly rows,
Her silky ringlets, jetty hue
O'er her fairneck their contrast threw;

6. *American Bench & Bar;* see Epilogue.

Her raven brow in arch praise,
Lent grace and lustre to her eyes;
Those sparkling orbs of purest blue,
Evinced a kindly heart and true;
Proportions of the fairest mould.

This is godawful verse, defiant in its wretchedness, but one could live with it, more or less, for a page or two. But what might one do with the following, in which Coffinberry strives for a sentimental effect through trying to reproduce his forest hero's dialect?

I used to live on the Kenawas
Till burnt out by the devlish 'Tawas,
They killed my wife, the poor, dear critter,
I never, never can forgit her.

This epic ends almost as badly, the attempt at frontier dialect abandoned:

Julia was all blushing in her charms,
Was given to her lover's arms.
And thus ended all the toils and dangers
Of these praiseworthy "Forest Rangers."

The article from which I gleaned this little harvest was published in *The Ohio Archaeological and Historical Society Publications,* vol. 10, written by N.B.C. Love, D.D., and titled "The Pioneer Poet Lawyer." I mention this fact because of the wonderfully diplomatic and ambiguous way in which Love ended his piece:

While a hundred years ago [this was published in 1902] there were those in the Northwest who wrote verses, most of which were the crudest doggerels, yet an occasional gem fell from their pens, but one only wrote an epic, Count Coffinberry. Critically, there is little to be said of the poem, it has faults and blemishes but it is correct in rhythm, accent, rhyme, and flows as gracefully along as the Miami of the Lakes [note: Coffinberry at this time was living in Perrysburg, near present-day Toledo] in the leafy month of June. (p. 314)

All we can hope is that Coffinberry's legal presence was more impressive than his poetry, and that his oratory in the courtroom was greater than this poetic sample suggests—even if he was defending a hog thief.

Epilogue

Readers who take footnotes seriously—and I am one—will have been waiting for clarification and fulfillment of the dereliction and promise in certain footnotes in this essay. Such readers deserve satisfaction. Footnotes are important not only insofar as they link one's text with larger dimensions of knowledge—they are intrinsically interesting. Their interest is, in fact, related to their importance; which is precisely as it should be.

There are a few occasions when footnotes provide most that is interesting in a treatise. Functioning as *obiter dicta,*[1] they provide a counterpoint to the melody of the text and are therefore possessed of their own music. Although I have never heard of anyone reading *only* the footnotes of a scholarly work, the idea is not entirely without the possibility of merit. What one would experience is not the work itself, but the aura of its nativity, along with some sample of at least part of its scholarly background.

This is not altogether an unattractive idea, and I may actually give it a shot sometime—read only the footnote melody of a book and see what sort of thrills it provides. I suspect the experience will prove much more rewarding than most of the avant-garde stories that are now so fashionable, consisting of paragraph probes that avoid the linkages we have long required in narrative, being naturally, humanly curious about how one thing leads to another. Learning what we can about causality in the human matrix is as important an enterprise as we can conceive, and our curiosity about such matters feeds upon the genius of fiction as narrative art. Conversely, the power of fiction to provide models of human causality is precisely what gives it its unique power and relevance.

But footnotes, like the ideals of scholarship itself, hardly need defending. Not even scholars need defending; although a great many who call themselves scholars are in grave need—and scholarly apparatus should never assume priority over enlightened or at

---

1. I am reminded, in this context, that the first word is cognate with *obituary*—both having to do with "passing": *obiter dicta,* as in "comments made in passing," which is to say, somewhat parenthetically, "by the way," and *obituary,* as in that other kind of passing, which as a young man I thought was a neologistic euphemism, but in the passage of years have learned has a much more ancient and learned heritage, so that when an older generation (the euphemism is much less common now) spoke of someone "passing away," they were speaking out of a heritage far older than I (and possibly they) realized.

least sensible discourse and honest testimony, which *are* the essence of scholarship. And whoever reads footnotes independent of the text should never pretend that he or she has experienced the text itself.

Now that we know something about footnotes and their relationship to the text, I am forced to explain the absence of what should be footnotes in *Books and Learning on the Frontier, God Help Us* (God help me!). This piece was first written for presentation at the opening of the pioneer museum at Hocking Technical College, in Nelsonville, Ohio. My contribution was meant to be read aloud, and that is what I did. The footnotes in the text were more obviously subsidiary and instrumental than they would have been if the piece had been explicitly directed toward publication.

In short, I proclaim that I know more or less how to make a footnote, which is something almost anybody can master. If there is an art to footnoting, it lies in the footnote text itself—in the language and style of what the footnote presents—and not in the conventionalized, minimally correct bibliographical information presented.

This is dangerous argumentation, to be sure. People who excuse themselves too readily from proper conventional forms are not to be trusted. I tell students this when I fancy they might be secretly proud of creative spelling; I tell them that in one sense, and among other things, spelling is a moral concern, for it makes a demand upon us by means of forms about which we are all expected to come together. (Such arguments automatically exempt dyslexics and others who may have innate problems in perceiving the *gestalten* of printed words—I am speaking here only of lazy and self-indulgent malingerers.)

As you will have noticed, I am having difficulty in working my way toward a confession that concerns the piece you have just read, along with those empty though promissory footnotes. I do not think my confession should be made, or taken, lightly. What I have to confess is that *I simply cannot find the sources of those quoted passages!* (There. Though somewhat diminished, I feel better already.)

I can assure you only of this: I have not dreamed those quoted passages. I have quoted those passages accurately, even though I cannot for the life of me name the authors of the books where I found them. I simply can't lay my hands on my copy of *American Bench and Bar*, from which I took the last quoted section. I have looked "everywhere," as they say, for my copy, and I can't find it. Why don't I seek out another? Well, I have tried, but according to the references I have consulted, it simply doesn't exist. It is not in our university's card catalogue, nor is it known by our computer, *Alice.* Even more astonishing, *The National Union Catalogue* doesn't list it; nor does *The British Museum Catalog.* I can't find traces of this book anywhere; and yet, I know that it exists, or did so at one time in the recent past, and that such was its title.

The other book is an even greater mystery. Why—even in the context of preparing an oral delivery—I did not bother to name and further identify my source, I'll never know. Why didn't I think ahead to the possibility of eventual publication? Like most writers, I often have my eye upon such a possibility. It is merely prudent, after all. But I was not prudent, and did not think ahead, and retrieving that title now is beyond my capacity. It has become part of that great preponderance of forgotten detail that is characteristic of my history as a human being.

Somewhere (don't ask me where),[2] William Lyon Phelps asserted that he had a brother who could actually remember every day of the last sixty years of his life, and upon being questioned (by someone who'd kept a diary, perhaps, or consulted a newspaper), would be able to give detailed and specific information about what he did or what happened on that day. This strikes me as a mixed blessing, if not something of a curse; but at this moment, in this context, I envy that man his phenomenal memory.

Now that the disgraceful facts have been disclosed, I'll close this Epilogue—which functions somewhat as a footnote, but will have, I think, a more graceful presence in its present posture of summary. Given the legal character of what has gone before, it seems only proper that I should end by stating that I have confessed my crime of scholarly negligence and hereby throw myself upon the mercy of the court.

---

2. *Memory,* (New York, 1929). "Inasmuch as, so far as I know, the gift [of virtually total recall] is unique, it may not be an impertinence to record the fact that my brother, the Reverend Doctor Dryden William Phelps, can recall some particular thing that has happened on any day during the last sixty years; and he can recall it immediately, upon demand, in response to any challenge" (pp. 5–7). The author has just referred to Lord Macaulay's verbatim recall of a long oration, "as if he were reading it" (p. 5).

The Library of Ignorance

**W**hile it is obviously impossible for a truly dedicated bibliophile ever to buy enough books to ease the great ache in his spirit, it is easy to buy too many for the lesser purpose of remembering when and where you got a particular volume. Or, more unsettling perhaps, how much you paid for it.

Appropriately, this is the case with a slender little book I own. It is bound in grayish-blue marbled boards, with cloth spine and paper labels, and bears the catchy title *The Library and the Librarian.* Its author was a man named Edmund Lester Pearson.

This book was published by The Elm Tree Press, in Woodstock, Vermont, in 1910. I'd never heard of Pearson or The Elm Tree Press either one. I'd heard of Woodstock—if it's the one I think it is—but any reference to *that* Woodstock would be wildly incompatible with what I know of the Edmund Lester Pearson who wrote this book.

As for the book, it is subtitled: "A selection of Articles from the Boston Evening Transcript and other Sources," and it is number two in "The Librarian's Series / Edited by / John Cotton Dana and Henry W. Kent." I didn't know any more about them than I did Edmund Lester Pearson, although I couldn't help wondering if Dana wasn't perhaps a grandson or maybe a great nephew of that other one. You know who.

When all of this is added to the fact that I have no idea when and where I bought the book, we have to conclude that we are in the presence of an impressive amount of ignorance. Or mind-deep in mystery, let us say. And even though I know I must have paid something for it (probably as part of an accumulation of several boxes purchased somewhere), the fact that I can't remember exactly how much I paid for this specific volume makes the book a sort of gift.

What makes it more of a gift is the fact that Edmund Lester Pearson, for all his powerful anonymity, was a writer. More than that, he was a good one. He had wit, he knew things, he cared about the world, and he understood the language and could make it cavort and purr with the style that separates a great animal trainer from the great majority who know just about enough to feed their pet collie.

Language as it is used by most writers is little more than an accumulation of words arranged according to syntactic conventions; but there is some prose that we think of as beautiful, emphasizing the fact by saying that it is alive. This metaphor can mean more than we usually mean *by* it; and if you take samples from such a living text, you will likely feel the life in it even there, in each fragment. Things that are alive consist of living cells, and so it is with the language when it is vital. Go to a living text and pluck out a few sentences: they will reveal their natural and pulsatile animation.

Since most of us enter a text at the beginning, we are alert for signs of life, as well as for the felt presence of a mind that will necessarily see the world in a unique and (if we're lucky) interesting perspective. Often, the opening sentence will cast a shadow over what follows, as in that famous instance: "None of them knew the color of the sky." This shadow-casting sentence opens Stephen Crane's story, "The Open Boat"—and what a twofold opening we have here!

Pearson's opening essay, on the other hand, titled "The Librarian in Fiction," is not the sort to open a reader's eyes. Or so you might think. But the beginning sentence bears a testimony so radically different from the title that the shock is considerable. "The librarian," Pearson begins, "has never played a thunderous part in history."

I am not about to lose myself in an ecstasy of appreciation because of a single sentence, even if it's the first. Like most readers, I make demands in intricate and ultimately inscrutable ways (i.e., I usually don't know what I want until I read it). I expect something of the next sentence, as well; and of the one after that.

However, as synecdoche, Pearson's opening sentence is a wry and winsome move. (Yes, there is an aesthetic chess game happening with every text, although the writer's great antagonist is a committee of cant, blithering, and silence, never the reader.) Pearson's sentence possesses its own thunder in the word "thunderous," and he shows us that he is not only witty, but understands the venerable and ancient art of litotes, which is no mean accomplishment for a writer who has chosen as his subject, "The Librarian in Fiction."

Pearson's thesis is admirably present, refracted kaleidoscopically in each period as his essay marches toward its end. This thesis is simple: he does not like what writers of fiction have done with librarians. He points out that librarians in novels are without exception file-thumbing nerds. (The diction here is not Pearson's, but mine, in a sort of free-wheeling translation.) "One writer," Pearson observes (without naming him), "has objected to the wide-awake kind, and pleaded for a return to the half-asleep and covered-with-moss sort of librarian; but he is a literary person, himself, and of course peculiar."

Lovely vengeance, here. Smashing. Every red-blooded novelist will rejoice in this condemnation of novelists, for he will see anyone but himself reflected in the mirror. Furthermore, the wit is still intact, and the stylishness of that thunderous opening has not diminished by even half a serif.

Pearson's documentation of what we would today call the "image" of the librarian as presented stereotypically and relentlessly in fiction is damning. Most of the novelists cited are by now unread and forgotten, which seems only fair in the present context.

One of the samples provided is a secret tippler—"the worst kind, without the excuse of conviviality"; another bears the first name of "Duodecimo" (his last is "Quarton"), significant of the fact he was a very small baby. Then there is the librarian whose mind is all thumbs, as evident in his or her classification of the *Autobiography of Leigh Hunt* under "Anonymous."

By now, the reader hates novelists as lovingly as novelists evidently used to hate librarians. I say "used to," because I have read an awful lot of novels published since 1910, and I can't remember a single character in any of them that was a librarian. But if I had come upon one, I suspect Pearson's thesis would be corroborated. All of which is very mysterious, for libraries are in their own way the most adventurous places in the world. No one who helps preside over them in any way, you would think, could remain completely unaffected by the adventure.

And in real life they are not. Pearson says so, and I believe him.

(He himself was a librarian, but his authorial authority makes this fact irrelevant.) Having sounded the *contra* in his essay, he now gives full voice to the *pro*, proclaiming that, contrary to the prejudicial testimony of novelists, librarians in real life are nothing less than human beings. If you prick them, they bleed. They even have their jests. It is true that these jests are not always of the better sort. In fact, the fourth saddest joke I have ever heard was told to me by a head librarian, who took his pen and on a sheet of paper drew a high, narrow capital letter "A." "What book is that?" he asked. I answered in a spirit of sturdy truthfulness that I didn't know. "In no sense 'A-Broad,' " he said, working his features up into a brief rictus to indicate that the jest was over.

Well, perhaps the novelists weren't *all* wrong. But we should not forget Pearson, who has still not had his say. Whom does he choose to represent those real librarians that belie the grotesque and unfair exaggerations of novelists? None other than Casanova, the Prince of Bedrooms.

So much is no more than the truth: Casanova ended his life as a librarian. *Post hoc ergo propter hoc?* Perhaps. Casanova had been busy all his life—not just with philandering and intrigue, but he had been a reader, as well. An intellectual. And having been so worldly for so long, it seems felicitous that he should retire to a library in late middle age, where he could spend his last years in thoughtful study, and maybe even learn something of what he had been up to all that time . . . something of "what it all meant."

Whatever his reasons for becoming a librarian, we know that the post was a good one, for it was in the service of Count Walstein in his castle in Bohemia. It is true that Casanova is not remembered in the way of that Dewey whose decimals entranced whole generations up until the Library of Congress era . . . whose generation's enchantment lasted only until the advent of a computer named Alice. Nor was he famous in the way of Panizzi, whose great monument is the British Museum. But he was a librarian.

Pearson might have added many other great names to his list of real librarians in a real world. In a way, it's a shame that chronology did not allow him to know of Lawrence Clark Powell, whose passion for books, scholarship, research, and collecting would give him a prominent role in helping to offset the dullness of Duodecimo Quarton and the exhaustion of the "exhausted librarian who seemed tacitly to echo the weary cry of King Solomon."

Pearson's book is only eighty-seven pages deep, but that is deep enough. One of the pieces bears the austere title, "098." What could such a title mean? What it labels is more story than essay, and more fantasy than either.

In it, Pearson (or the narrator) is approached in his lodgings by a stranger who invites him to come see his book collection. A harmless-enough request, especially in view of the fact that the man identifies himself as a neighbor. It turns out that he even lives in the same building.

The narrator agrees and gets on the elevator (we must think 1910 here, visualizing a wrought-iron, cagelike contraption with pulleys and long, serpentine, slowly dancing cables). But the elevator—like many of its devilish kind (I think of Par Lagerkvist's "The Lift that Went Down to Hell")—does not descend merely to the ground floor or basement . . . it keeps on going.

Eventually, it stops, and the two men get off and enter a comfortable and bookish apartment. There, the bibliophile begins to show off his prime possessions, among which are such titles as *The True Precepts of the Dramatick Art,* by William Shakespeare; the prompt book of *Hamlet,* with the author's annotations and directions for stage business; a letter from Shakespeare to Burbage; a copy of Marlowe's *Edward II,* stained with his own blood from the fatal tavern duel; a five-act play written by John Milton; Lee's "lost dispatch—found two days before Antietam and sent to McClellan." (This last was wrapped around three cigars—the man who found it smoked two of them, but the mysterious book collector owned the other, and had it right there with him in the basement's basement.)

"I did not believe him," the narrator states rather stuffily, referring to the nonexistent play by Milton, "but again it was, if not genuine, a very laborious hoax, indeed."

And delicious stuff, indeed. The climax for the reader who is also a book collector comes near the end, where climaxes ought to be. The mysterious bibliophile holds up two copies of Johnson's *Dictionary,* saying, "One of them is the identical copy that Becky Sharp flung out of the carriage when she left school. The other stood on Nelson's writing desk in his cabin on the Victory."

Older readers will understand the title more readily than the young, for in Dewey's famous classification, 098 is the section devoted to "Imaginary Books" . . . which, as we all know, glow with the light that never was on sea or land.

The world of books is wonderfully complex, and the number of titles that populate it seems to be as nearly infinite as the number of stars. Or consider the fossilized metaphor of a book's *leaves:* are the number of leaves of all the books extant equivalent to the number of real leaves on real trees in the world?

While you are figuring this out, I will go on to state that the variety and extensiveness of the world of books are part of its challenge, its openness, its adventurousness. The frontier of the Old West was nothing like it, for that frontier—like all others—is partly contained in the world of books; while this secondary world contains its own sorts of reality, much of which differs from the superstition of atomic historical fact as dramatically as a Mozart quartet differs from the valves of a trumpet.

Think of all the rich characters and powerful scenes that no one has read for years, perhaps centuries; think of the utterances lying in that darkness where all old books accumulate, awaiting some nudge toward rebirth that might illuminate your existence.

While I obviously believe that all of the above insights are true and worth making, it is also the case that they are an oblique approach to my confession that Edmund Lester Pearson is not, or should not be, all that anonymous. I am certain that many scholarly librarians and book collectors know of him, and some no doubt know his work well. He is not all that obscure a writer, and one of his books has even been reprinted within the past few years (*The Librarian,* Scarecrow Press, 1976).

As a matter of fact, he was a writer of acknowledged distinction, not simply a figure of undeserved neglect. The things he wrote about are of particular interest to book collectors, for Pearson was one of us. Furthermore, some of his books are proved "collectibles"; for example, I note that his *The Old Librarian's Almanack* (published pseudonymously by "Philobiblos" in Woodstock, Vt., in 1909) sold for $35 at auction in 1978. This book is a hoax, pretending to be a "very rare pamphlet first published in New Haven Connecticutt in 1773 and now reprinted for the first time" (shades of "098" and the prompt book for *Hamlet*).

Pearson was a bibliophile in the grand old manner, and published books on crime and book collecting (not always clearly distinguishable). Some of his other titles are *The Secret Book, Books in Black or Red,* and *Dime Novels.* As a scholar, he was ahead of his time in his interest in popular culture and popular fiction. In short, Pearson had a certain fame, and I should have known about him. If I had the energy, I'd be ashamed of myself.

And yet, my chagrin is not unlimited. Pearson himself was capable of error, as revealed in his volume titled *Queer Books* (a title he would change to *Eccentric Books* today). In the chapter, "Making the Eagle Scream" (about Fourth of July oratory), he wrote: "Robert Y. Hayne was eminent enough in his day, but the place he occupies in American history is what is known in the variety theatre as the "straight man" or "feeder." Nobody knows what he said, on a certain famous occasion, but everyone knows what Daniel Webster said in reply."

This passage is footnoted with information cheerfully provided by Pearson, that a descendent of Hayne wrote to him after the essay was first printed, accusing him of "withering ignorance" in not knowing who his ancestor was.

I am encouraged by this footnote and the tone in which it is noted; I rejoice in Pearson's magnanimity, knowing that he would have forgiven my not knowing who he was. He might have pointed out that he didn't know who *I* was, either, and chronology be damned.

We who are withered by ignorance should stand together, independent of the dates of our insertion into history or what used to be called "The Passing Parade."

In that by-now famous essay that begins *The Library and the Librarian*, Pearson neglects to mention the most interesting of all fictional references to a librarian. At the beginning of *Moby Dick*, on the page titled "Extracts / (Supplied by a Sub-Sub-Librarian.)," there is a section consisting of two paragraphs, equally balanced. In the first, the Sub-Sub-Librarian is addressed as "painstaking burrower and grubworm of a poor devil of a Sub-Sub," and then reminded of the hopelessness of his working through all the references to whales in the books that had accumulated up to that time, 1850 A.D. (The world's supply of books has probably tripled or quadrupled since that time; but even then, the Sub-Sub's task was Sisyphean.)

But read the second paragraph, valedictorian after the mock pity of the first:

So fare thee well, poor devil of a Sub-Sub, whose commentator I am. Thou belongest to that hopeless, sallow tribe which no wine of this world will ever warm; and for whom even Pale Sherry would be too rosy-strong; but with whom one sometimes loves to sit, and feel poor-devilish, too; and grow convivial upon tears; and say to them bluntly, with full eyes and empty glasses, and in not altogether unpleasant sadness—Give it up, Sub-Subs! For by how much the more pains ye take to please the world, by so much the more shall ye for ever go thankless! Would that I could clear out Hampton Court and the Tuileries for ye! But gulp down your tears and hie aloft to the royal-mast with your hearts; for your friends who have gone before are clearing out the seven-storied heavens, and making refugees of long-pampered Gabriel, Michael, and Raphael, against your coming. Here ye strike but splintered hearts together—there, ye shall strike unsplinterable glasses!

One reason for Pearson's not quoting this lyric exordium might be that it runs counter to his thesis, for the poor sallow drab of a Sub-Sub verges somehow upon being grand and majestic, even as he remains pathetic and comic. In this brief paragraph, we can see the shadow of Bartleby the Scrivener, who contains all the mystery any human can carry in his soul, even if the unread tomes of centuries weigh upon his memory. Dead letters all.

Melville's large sympathy is nowhere more evident than in that apostrophe to the Sub-Sub-Librarian, and it is merely justice that this should be so. For where would Melville have gotten his mighty book except from the mighty books of the dead, collated with what was once termed the *Book of Nature?* That Ahab's creator was a prodigious reader is amply proved by the discovery, some years ago, of Melville's signature on library cards from various places, showing how much he devoured . . . and incidentally proving, by their great descent upon the records of all possible libraries, how relentless dealers and collectors can be.

My theme, however, is not libraries or librarians, nor is it the writing of Edmund Lester Pearson. It is not astonishing that I knew nothing about him until by chance I somehow got his book, *The Library and the Librarian,* and started to read it. I am old enough and have learned enough not to be surprised by evidence of how much I don't know. And it is this, a sense of knowing where to feel the full weight of one's ignorance . . . *this* is what I'm after, and have been from the start. Sensed ignorance is the frontier of knowledge, always—therefore, the place of adventure and challenge.

For this purpose, Edmund Lester Pearson serves as a means; and therefore plays an important and noble part. He and his work are both symbol and sample of my theme, which is the great world of things observed, felt, remembered, and imagined, as it can be found in old books. There are many writers whose works are forgotten or only vaguely remembered who can enliven us. While it is true that most of what has been written in the past is trivial, silly, or the labored product of intense mediocrity (just like most that is being written, thought, and sensed today; relevance is a trap, after all, and it always has been), there are nevertheless those few who have managed in various ways to escape and have therefore been unjustly forgotten. There are truths waiting for us in the pages of forgotten works that cannot be found in the world around us.

Consider, by contrast, the hysterical yea-saying that accompanies what is termed the "electronic revolution" or "the advent of the computer age." Everyone joins in the chorus, which fact in itself makes the enterprise questionable: with such a consensus, something *has* to be wrong.

And the truth is, this greatly lauded and sickeningly hyped phenomenon has produced absolutely nothing to advance or enhance the humanizing clarity, geniality, and perspective that characterize Pearson's work and make it worth reading. The fact that technology has made it possible to produce more books more swiftly merely increases the rate of textual reproduction (including typographical errors), and will impress no one who hasn't already abdicated his intelligence to the superstitions of mass and topicality; such "advances" have had no effect whatsoever upon the quality of mind that was required for Pearson's writing such books and that will always be to some extent required for understanding what he is saying.

Only consider: will any conceivable sort of electronic gadgetry prove useful in understanding the subtleties of language and custom implicated in the works of Anthony Trollope or Henry James? Could anybody seriously argue that the availability of such electronic means would have enlarged or enriched their own clear and complex visions of life? D. H. Lawrence wrote that the novel was the best model we have of the complexities of human interconnectedness; and the silicon chip, with all its stupendous power, hasn't provided any sort of reason to affect or modify Lawrence's statement.

The world of printed books is half a millennium old, and all but the last one-twentieth of that period produced books by letterpress in one form or other. The electronic revolution has done nothing to invalidate the old truths, just as it has not provided any new means for exposing any of the old idiocies that have always permeated, and probably always will permeate, the human condition. The means for exposing such idiocies are as old as Socrates, and they are built into the language as surely as the means for clear and lofty thought are built into it, coeval and yet living, which is to say, capable of change and growth.

As books continue to be printed—even by photo-offset from the latest and most advanced electronic virtuosity—their population grows. Just as it is a shame that I didn't know anything about Edmund Lester Pearson and how he saw the world about him, so it would be shameful if there were not people somewhere committed to the irrelevance of reading old books and learning to understand what is said in them.

English departments of colleges and universities and, to some extent, public schools, are in the business of institutionalizing literature. If every book assigned in English classes throughout the land over the past ten years were eliminated, a viable curriculum of currently "unknown books" could replace them and provide a valid curriculum. And if that curriculum were destroyed, still a third would be waiting. This is not to argue that literary works do not differ in merit, or that literary/aesthetic principles have no validity . . . merely that we have an intrinsic need for stories and poems, and can adjust to what's available and be nourished by it.

A generation ago, no college freshman could ever become a sophomore without having read (or at least, having had assigned in one of his classes) two books: *Walden* and *Huckleberry Finn.* Today, half of the nation's college seniors will have read the latter, and only a very small percentage will even have heard of Thoreau's *magnum opus.*

Is this to be taken as an index of sagging standards or galloping illiteracy? Not simply. But today, the assignments tend toward more "relevant" literature (yes, the idea still hangs on, though the shibboleth has become virtually inaudible): *Catch 22, The Golden Notebook,* and *Play It as It Lays.*

As a practicing novelist and short-story writer, I'm not about to find fault with assigning the work of living writers; and I've gone on record as admiring Pearson's courageous and insightful work with popular Literature in a day when such materials were judged *infra dig* by just about everybody.[1]

But somebody, or some of us some of the time, should be scanning old books, looking for a part of the world that has been forgotten or perhaps never really understood. This means reading the classics, even, for they too fall into the abyss of silence. When was the last time you even *heard* of somebody reading something by Charles Lamb, Sir Walter Scott, or Tobias Smollett?

And then there are all those anonymous Edmund Lester Pearson's waiting to be discovered, by chance, or perhaps cued by some such enthusiastic report as this I am laboring to close. Book collectors are the right sort of people for such adventures, of course. And the fact that not one in a hundred of the authors we test will prove as fine and luminous a writer as Pearson should not inhibit us in the least. When we are scanning, or sampling, a text—or giving way to it and reading for pleasure—we don't have anybody to please but ourselves, and we can put down the product of a drone, sausage wit, or whistle head without the least nudge of guilt.

But always that one percent is waiting. And one percent of the books a person can pick up and leaf through is an awesome population. The wisdom and joy one might come upon will be old, in the nature of things—for print always comes to us from the past; but it will be new, as well, for even the old and discarded treasures will appear to us in the light of the world around us, which has never existed before.

This means that those texts have never existed before, either. They are waiting to be found out and read. They lurk somewhere in darkened rooms all about us, a library we don't know about, a library of ignorance. And when you think about it, isn't the promise of their discovery a fine and lovely thing?

---

1. In his *Dime Novels,* Pearson sardonically points out that sometimes four or five centuries are required for popular literature to be accepted and taken seriously.

Arenas of Books

The excitement and adventure of a book sale are like nothing else. I am speaking of the kind of sale sponsored by local chapters of the AAUW, Friends of Library groups (either public or university), and the annual sales of such charitable groups as the Twig, whose proceeds all go to children's hospitals.

These sales generally begin at 9:00 A.M., and I always try to be there an hour early. Usually, I am either first or second in line. If I am second, the person before me is likely to be Bob Roe, an old booking friend whose scholarly tastes don't seriously overlap my own: he collects modern books on the development of American speech and medieval studies, and his collection of second printings of Faulkner, Hemingway, and Fitzgerald is, to the best of my knowledge, unrivaled. But then, one would be hard put to identify any competition for second printings. Bob is the sort of friend you like to go booking with, or find waiting ahead of you in line when you arrive an hour early.

One pays a price for everything, of course; and arriving an hour early for an AAUW sale in Chillicothe, which is an hour's drive from my house, means I have to leave at 6:30 A.M., allowing me a half-hour's stop for breakfast. Most people are not willing to rise so early to attend a book sale. They deserve the third printings, bound Reader's Digests, and book club editions that will be waiting for them. But then, most people won't drive fifty miles or more to attend a book sale, no matter what the hour; they don't know what they're missing.

A sort of camaraderie grows among those of us who do arrive early. We are pretty much the same group, so that if for some reason one of us doesn't show up before sale time, we ask about him or her. "Where's Paul?" Or "Why isn't Karen here?" When we aren't asking such questions, we are talking about books—about finding a copy of an eighteenth-century broadside in an attic, or perhaps a first edition of *The Aspern Papers* at a barn sale. While we are waiting, often in the cold (such sales are not usually held in the summer), the women inside—those in charge—get things ready. They put up signs in the proper places, announcing "Fiction" and "History," plug in their adding machines, see that there is plenty of tape, and count change in the cigar boxes at the checkout tables. They also occasionally glance up and smile (a little nervously, I sometimes fancy), for they know us almost as well as we know one another. If one of the helpers arrives late, she has to crowd past those of us who are standing in line, a gauntlet of badinage. Almost always it is women who do this work—I'm not sure why. Perhaps an eleemosynary nudge in the female hormone. Most book collectors, on the other hand, are men. The mystery abides.

One of the most beguiling features of sales such as these is the cheapness of their books. Those women are there to do business on behalf of their organization, and as the old television commercial put it: they can be very friendly. Books are usually marked at garage sale prices, a quarter or half-dollar, except for a few that are put aside on a "gem table," with prices of a dollar or more. Sometimes there is a "silent bid" table, a thing I always hate to see. I don't want to wait; if I buy a book, I want it now, and I want to know immediately whether I've bought it or not.

The inescapable fact is, these ladies—intelligent readers all, but innocent in the dark arts of pricing rare books—don't know what they're doing, and the gem table seldom has anything like the bargains that can be found in the slush.

These women don't know, nor should they. If their sales are honestly conducted, they will occasionally provide such lustrous bargains for the customers that they will not only drive a hundred miles, but arrive an hour early so they can peek through the glass doors to see how the sale is shaping up.

Sometimes, when those in charge are haunted by the specter of "lost profits," they will call in a dealer and ask that the books be priced somewhat according to their potential retail value in an antiquarian bookstore. The dealer is usually paid "in kind"—allowed to pick out a box for himself—unless he or she can be enlisted as a volunteer, too.

But more often than not, strategies like this are simply a means for outwitting themselves: if there are no bargains, the time will soon come when there will be no crowding about the doors an hour early. Think of the 100 or more miles driven to get there, and the cost of a breakfast of hot cakes and sausage necessary for the arduous task of squatting under tables as you fumble through books and heft boxes filled with treasures up to the checkout table. Book collectors are, more than most, vulnerable to folly; but even we can draw the line if we are repeatedly denied bargains where bargains are meant to be.

There are strategies to be considered, of course. I remember many years ago when my son, then fourteen, and I arose at 2:00 A.M., got in our recently purchased Vega station wagon (a second car that I considered ideal for such booking trips), and started out for St. Louis, where the Brandeis University Alumni Book Sale was scheduled to begin at six o'clock in the evening.

After hard driving, we arrived at four o'clock—two hours before gate time—and found two lines already queuing up at the guarded entrances of a huge, open-sided circus tent, whose shadowy interior contained tables piled with 100,000 books. One line had about twenty people in it; the other only two. I couldn't understand this disproportion then, and still can't. My son and I made numbers three and four in the second queue, which I didn't think was too bad, considering the long drive.

I had heard of this sale for years, how good it was, how vast a profusion of books were periodically unloaded over the heads and shoulders of perspiring bibliophiles as they hauled in their manifold treasures. Naturally, I was excited. The line behind us grew, along with the line beside us, until both reached back over two hundred yards, where they disappeared around the corners of buildings. Once the sale started, the pressure from the rear would be formidable, and there would be no easy way to turn back, or stroll to another area—at least during the critical early stages of the sale.

Now I was faced with an interesting problem: I had to try to judge the sophistication of those in charge. This is a familiar nuance in every strategy: how much does your opponent know? How cunning is he? Or *she?* Essential to the theory of games is the principle of incomplete information.

Some thirty yards before me, to the right, was a table filled with books, and above it there was a large sign with the words RARE BOOKS clearly printed on it. Did those who'd organized this sale *know* rare books? As I've said, this is not often the case. Should I commit myself to this table, which was a good distance from those labeled "Literature" and "Fiction" and "History"?

I decided to go to the slush; I reasoned that if so many books had been segregated as "rare" by an expert, they would be priced accordingly, somewhere near their theoretical retail value—and if they had not been judged by an expert, the label meant nothing. Moreover, having gotten up at two in the morning for this sale, I felt I should risk everything with the idea of coming upon truly gorgeous, splendid, succulent, irresistible bargains. Or even better.

But it appears I was mistaken, for the sale was a poor one, so far as I was concerned. C−, let's say. I did, of course, buy two or three boxes of books (I certainly wasn't going to go through all that for nothing), but the prize was hardly worth getting up at 2:00 A.M. and driving over 600 miles for, even at a quarter a volume.

Was the "rare book" table in truth filled with rare books? If I had that sale to live over again, I'd change my strategy and find out; but as it is, I have no way of finding out, nobody to phone and ask. Those queues were filled with strangers, except for a dealer friend who'd come all the way from Wichita—almost as distant in the other direction as Athens, Ohio. Still, I didn't see her afterwards to ask how she'd done. Nor did I phone. I don't think I could have borne the news that a first edition of *Barchester Towers* had been picked up on the rare book table for $10.00.

I suspect that the books had been gone over very carefully, perhaps knowledgeably, and most or all of the rarities had been culled out. I'll not go to so much trouble to attend that particular sale again, although there have been sales I *have* attended that would get me out of bed at 2:00 A.M. any day of the year, even with snow falling and a threat of nuclear attack.

Devising my own strategies and tactics, I have, of course, borne witness to those employed by others. I have seen dealers bring their whole families, perhaps reaching as far as second cousins, schooling them assiduously in the general varieties of book that should be grabbed up. Later, the entire clan will gather around their island of loot while the knowledgeable ones examine the haul more carefully, rejecting the unworthy and boxing up their purchases. I have seen dealers with surplus navy duffel bags hold them open at the end of a table and scoop an entire row of books into it. This is not being as selective as one might be, but then it is a tactic, of sorts, and is no doubt possessed of some virtue.

Certain proprieties do obtain, however. The powerful covenant implicit in the act of "queuing up" is manifest here, as elsewhere. Occasionally someone will try to break into the line—to "ditch," as we once called it in the cafeteria lines at school—but such ugly types are seldom successful, and it is only right that they fail. Occasionally, someone will come to the head of a line to talk with a friend, and there is always the suspicion he might pretend to forget himself at the last moment and find his body carried in on the vanguard of the attack, so that he is forced to throw himself upon the fresh stock along with those who have more earnestly worked for the privilege.

But as the starting time approaches, a certain hostility can be felt, even by those who are sufficiently insensitive to consider such a ploy; and the friendly intruder eventually makes his way back to the end of the line, if it is in sight. Or perhaps he goes back home to sulk and spend an hour in idle regret that he did not rise earlier.

When someone tries to break into the line, he or she crosses a less visible line, tacitly accepted by the majority, and is thereby in danger of arousing the wrath of those who play the game fairly. This is taboo, of course, and otherwise gentle folk can become exasperated. Upon occasion I myself have physically barred the obtrusive entrance of this particular type of nerd, and I have yet to find one who will fight back. The proprieties, while invisible, are in truth strong.

Is it any wonder that, after witnessing such behavior, one should begin to have fantasies? I am still speaking of strategies and tactics, and am compelled to admit that there is one scenario that holds a morbid and abiding fascination for me. This scenario is vivid, specific, and characterized by a low and shameful cunning.

It begins with my hiring a strong old actress with a loud voice. Not just any strong old actress with a loud voice will do: this woman will have to be skilled in the arts of turmoil, panic, and confusion. I will have her dressed in black taffeta; and perhaps, for her own security, she will wear a veil.

She will be expected to take her place directly behind me in line one hour before the announced opening of a sale. I will be first, of course. The sale we are thinking of must be one in which an admission charge of, say, two dollars will be required; and there must be only one entrance to the sale area. I will provide this woman with a single $100 bill, and she will have no other money in her purse. I, you will correctly surmise, will have the exact change ready in my pocket. When the starting gun is fired (metaphor here; for I have never actually heard a gun fired at such a time), I will descend upon the books alone, untroubled by even the most vaporous thoughts of competition.

The woman I have employed will be lodged securely in the doorway, demanding change for her $100 bill. If others try to ease past her, the umbrella she is carrying will spring open, pinioning those within range. She will righteously insist upon not relinquishing her place in line, even as the pressure mounts. Perhaps she will start screaming in Yugoslavian, Turkish, or some hitherto unknown tongue.

I can almost hear the uproar and confusion, even feel them, for they would be palpable. I can see those tables covered with books, and not one other person to get in my way, except for a few bewildered lady attendants wearing their little badges or aprons and with lead pencils stuck in their hairdos, watching me as I buy at leisure— uninhibited, untroubled, and unharried.

Something a little like this actually happened to me once, when I casually stopped in a theological seminary down south and asked if they had any old or discarded books I might purchase. The woman stared at me a moment, and then led me downstairs and escorted me into a room filled with old books, saying they were just about to have a sale, and I could go ahead and help myself, since the books were all priced and waiting.

It was here, I recall, that I bought a first edition copy of William Darby's *A Tour to the Michigan Territory,* published in New York in 1819. And there were other bargains, similarly old and rare. I was all alone in that room, and I swear I could hear music. And I didn't even have to hire a crazy actress with a trick umbrella to keep out those who are less desirous, if not less deserving, for there was no one else around.

Buy why, in this baroque fantasy, a crazy actress with an umbrella instead of a man? I have thought about this and conclude that we are all very much alike, after all, and as I try to imagine myself caught behind someone blocking my way to old books containing God-knows-what unexpected treasures and rarities, I realize that I could never hit a woman, no matter what the provocation; whereas if a man blocked my way, I would probably attack him. Never mind how imprudent or undignified this would appear—these are old books we are talking about. Neither size nor youth would protect him, and I wouldn't be fooled by that $100 bill gimmick for two seconds.

No, it would have to be a woman, and she would have to be—as I have argued—very carefully selected. She would have to be solid on her feet and not subject to panic in the face of abuse. She would have to be a great actress, in a way, capable of playing the role of accomplice in a particularly grubby scene. And of course, she herself could not possibly be a book collector, for if she were, I couldn't trust her to carry out my orders.

Nevertheless, the world is safe from this particular scam, so far as I'm concerned. For one thing, it would be too expensive; the rewards from most sales wouldn't float such a venture. But there is a more important reason: it wouldn't be playing the game. The passion of bibliophily can tempt us into grotesque postures, no doubt, but the true book collector is, after all, an idealist; and even in the midst of strategies that might seem better fitted to the worlds of diplomacy or simple commerce, something of this idealism remains to taint his plans and inhibit him before commiting the grossest deceits.

For it *is* a game, of course; and the antagonist is not simply another mortal—there really isn't much glory in outwitting someone else, who may be feeling sleepy or bilious or possessed of a more complex view towards the ethical substructure of pure winning . . . the real antagonist is far more vaporous, sly, and elusive: the real antagonist can hardly be personified, as a matter of fact, for it is the world of chance. This is truly worthy of one's serious and attentive deliberations, for chance cannot even be defined mathematically, let alone bibliophilically in the context of a rich and teeming world of volumes that contains more than could ever seem to exist at one time to any one of us.

And of course chance is the essential ingredient of all great adventures, including the sort I have been describing.

Bits and Pieces

In the summer of 1980 I taught at the Jesse Stuart Writers' Conference in Murray, Kentucky—a three-week course that allowed for two full weekends of leisure in what was for my wife and me new and fresh booking country. Near the end of our first week, we bought all the local newspapers as well as those we could find from nearby regions, and studied the classified sections carefully.

I had run an ad in the local paper, with a box number, advertising for books, but there was no response waiting when I stopped in shortly after my arrival in Murray. We had also managed to check out all the local antique shops in Murray during my off-hours from teaching at the conference. Nothing.

But in one of the papers we consulted there was a notice of a large sale of household goods at an auction house just north of Paris, Tennessee—which made it just south of Murray and the Kentucky border. The auction was scheduled for 7:00 P.M., Friday, so we consulted our map and managed to arrive there an hour early.

There were at least twenty boxes of boxes, and a significant percentage seemed to have to do with the circus. Evidently someone's collection. Having no interest in the circus, I nevertheless showed my driver's license, got my ticket, lighted a cigar, and settled down to wait for the books to come up. It was a comfortable old building that might have been a church or school house at one time. But now it was an auction barn.

The auctioneer sounded just right: he sounded exactly like the Tennessee auctioneers used to sound on the radio in the Lucky Strike commercials when they'd end with "Sold, American!"—the

only words that could be understood, in spite of the fact that they say you should be able to recognize every word a good auctioneer chants, no matter how fast he goes.

Tennessee tobacco auctioneers have a sing-song delivery that I haven't heard anywhere else. Not that I haven't missed a lot of auctions; but I've attended a lot, too; and I've even heard a woman auctioneer work, which struck me as *contra naturam*, somehow— prejudice, no doubt. We also once heard an auctioneer work in the back country of Norway, and you could have read a short paragraph of stately prose between some of his utterances. I'll never forget his soporific *Fem og Femty* (55 kroner) as he sought to raise the price on a little wooden clock. But I can't remember what it actually brought: I think I was snoring by then.

But to return to Paris, Tennessee: I managed to get all the boxes of books that I wanted, for only two or three dollars a box. I went through them right there on my seat (they were piled about me on the floor and nearby chairs—the attendance was small) and culled out about one-eighth of all I'd bought. The rest I gave to one of the antique dealers from Murray, whom we recognized because we had visited his shop two days before. We had to be selective, because our car would not hold too many boxes, and we were a long way from home.

The most interesting thing I found, however, was not a book at all: it was a mint dust jacket of Steinbeck's *The Grapes of Wrath*. Furthermore, the dust jacket itself states "First Edition"—the only dust jacket I know that does this, as if in anticipation (corroborated) of many printings and considerable collecting interest. Often a dust jacket will have something like "Second Printing" on it—or "Third Large Printing"—but I know of no other that labels it as the first.

But where was the book that should go with it? Nowhere among all those circus books, and nowhere among the rejects. (Yes, I kep the circus books, and have since sold and traded most of them— although I still have half a ream of stationery, envelopes and letter heads both, of a circus museum located somewhere in Wisconsin How did this all get here? A question often asked, seldom ar swered.)

A mint dust jacket of a collectible book is a worthy acquisition even without the book itself. Still, I was more likely to pick up good copy of *The Grapes of Wrath* without dj than to come upo another dj with or without the book. Such are the probabilities.

And sure enough, within six months I bought a first edition of tl

book, minus dj, for 50¢. It was among some unmarked gift dupli-
cates at a small town library in Indiana. I then performed a mar-
riage, of sorts, bringing together two disparate parts of a single
book, so that now I have a mint copy in mint dj of Steinbeck's most
famous book—just as if the two of them had always lived together.

It doesn't often happen this way. When parts of a single title are
separated, the divorce is almost always final. There is a terrible
centrifugation at work in the careers of odd volumes. What Fate has
parted, no one can bring together again. At least, hardly ever.

For this reason, most sensible collectors very early in their careers vow not to buy odd volumes under any circumstances. Shelf
space is too precious, and the frustration of having an incomplete
set—whether it's one volume of two, or four out of five—is too
relentless a nagging in the back of one's mind. Life is interesting
enough without such ghosts to haunt us.

To abide by such a rule is a test of character, but it's one I consistently fail. I have accumulated boxes of orphaned volumes, knowing that even if I should happen upon a mate for one of them, it will
not likely have the same binding or the same degree of wear. The
matter is complicated by the fact that books are often bound incon-
sistently and even carelessly. This has always been so. The first
edition of *Moby Dick* comes in practically every color of the rain-
bow; and the first edition of Washington Irving's two-volume *The
Rocky Mountains* can be found in at least two colors, blue and tan.

This latter fact I know from personal experience for Irving's great
book digested from Captain Bonneville's journal is one of only two
two-volume editions I've ever matched. I've gotten two copies of
the same volume (e.g., two first volumes of Hawthorne's *The Mar-
ble Faun*) several times (Fate working diabolically, tantalizingly
here); but the first edition of Irving's *The Rocky Mountains* (Phila.,
1837) is one of only two sets I've ever actually matched. Each
volume has the required map; both volumes show similar (rather
heavy) wear; both have the fly leaves . . . however, my first volume
is in blue cloth, and my second volume is in tan.

What is my mismatched copy "worth"? I'm not sure. A matched
copy of the first edition is a very desirable western Americana title,
worth about $500 in fine condition, in spite of Howes's *US-iana* (2d
edition, 1962) labeling it as only an "a" item, meaning a value of
$10 to $25 at that time. But that time is long past, and Howe's
evaluation was probably too low, even then.

Bits and Pieces

The fact is, however, regardless of monetary value, I don't want to sell my copy; nor would I if the volumes were matched and in better shape. Furthermore, I take comfort in the fact that my chances are now substantially greater—ignoring the factor of wear—than they were before I matched/mismatched the second volume to the first.

How much greater, precisely? Easy to speculate, providing there were, in fact, only blue and tan bindings for the first edition (both Howes and Merle Johnson are silent, here); and if these were somewhat evenly distributed, then the chances of matching my first volume with the "right" second volume each time I came upon a single volume from the first edition were one out of four. That is, I could have gotten the blue 1st volume (the "same"), or the tan first volume (the same, different binding), or the blue second volume (the right, true mate), or the tan second volume (the mismatched mate I did in fact get). Now, of course, my chances are precisely doubled—that is, I can match my set from either direction: I can get a tan first volume, or a blue second volume, which presents me with two out of four possibilities for any odd volume of the first edition I come across. I'm getting closer, and the next move forward will be mate, for there's no way I can increase the probability of success to, say, 75 percent. Not in this world.

But such contemplations provide arid comfort. Of course, I'll keep looking, and looking hard; but I'd do this, anyway, even if I didn't have either volume. I'm obviously closer to filling that particular set than I was before; but I'm still a good distance away. One option available is for me simply to have both volumes rebound. They'd make a handsome set, in spite of the considerable foxing of the pages and slight tears (with no parts missing) in the maps. Foxing isn't much of a blemish in my personal view; I think of it pretty much as antique furniture lovers think of patina—if it doesn't make the text hard to read, it is merely the shadow of age, and adds to the book's character, as wrinkles can enhance a face.

The only other two-volume edition I've been able to "match" is Jeremy Belknap's *American Biography,* which is listed by Howes as follows:

Belknap, Jeremy
  American Biography . . . B 1794–8. 0 2v;
416; /4/ 476 aa
—rptd. N Y 1843. 18° 3 v: 370; 333; 315

This is perfectly clear, one would think. The first edition was published in Boston in two volumes, volume one in 1794 and volume two in 1798. (Belknap had died before the second volume was issued, but this does not affect the bibliography.)

Having picked up a copy of the second volume in boards many years ago, I advertised for a copy of volume one and was pleased to receive a quote for it at $25.00. This was a marginally high price, given the uncertainties of an acceptable match in wear (two volumes each labeled "fine" can vary significantly from each other) . . . and also given Howes's fairly modest evaluation of it ("aa" is his code for a book in the $25 to $100 range).

Still, Belknap's book is desirable (in it he tells the story of Madoc, the twelfth-century Welsh prince who was supposed to have reached America—although most of his information comes from Hakluyt, as he himself states), and the chances against matching an odd volume are so great that it seemed insensitive, somehow, to ignore such an opportunity. So I sent off my check, and volume one did in fact arrive: in good condition, excepting a broken hinge, as advertised . . . however, the book was bound in leather, while mine was in boards; furthermore, it is evident that while both volumes were printed from the same set of plates, my original volume two is a larger paper edition, and therefore a full inch higher than the other.

Howes did not mention such an edition, or I might have been wary; but obviously here is one of the rare instances in which Howes, like Homer, nods.

I have continued to advertise for missing volumes of various broken sets, but with no further luck. I have advertised generally ("interested in buying odd volumes of two- and three-volume sets of books printed in the U.S. or England before 1860") and specifically: "Wanted: Vol. I, only, of Christian Schultz's *Travels on an Inland Voyage through the States of New York, Pennsylvania, Virginia, Ohio, Kentucky and Tennessee*, New York, 1810."

Schultz's book is the only one that evoked a response, but it wasn't exactly what I needed. A man wrote saying that he also had the second volume, and if I got two quotations for the first, would I get in touch with him so that he could buy it from me? Indeed, I would have. (Past tense subjunctive; contrary-to-fact clause.) I would have, had I gotten a first offer of a first volume. But I did not; and there the matter rests, for the time being, with the second volume of Schultz's classic early narrative (rich with Mississippi

River lore) moldering on the shelf. It is still a good book to have, with an early map of the Ohio River, showing mostly empty space on both sides, but dutifully marking Wheeling, Marietta, Point Pleasant, "Galliopolis" (the only place I've seen that spelling), Cincinnati, Louisville, and Smithtown, between the mouths of the Tennessee and Cumberland rivers. A shy little rectangle on the left side of this map shows "Louisiana," which was at that time the name for all of that Terra Incognita west of the Mississippi.

Sometimes a book appears to be incomplete, but in fact is not. Occasionally, the "first" volume of a projected work is written and published, and for a variety of reasons—poor sales, sudden impoverishment, the author's death or loss of inspiration—no second volume will ever appear. This happens more frequently than one would suppose, especially in local history imprints which are often the repositories of primary source material and therefore valuable. I have never known a second volume to appear without a first, but I don't doubt the possibility, in view of the waggishness of authors, printers, and publishers generally. (This is almost the case with Poe's *Poems,* New York, 1831—the first edition of which states "Second Edition" on the title page; but of course, this isn't exactly the same.) Then, too, there is the possibility that a second or subsequent volumes will be printed in far greater numbers than the first, and that virtually all, or literally all, copies of the first have disappeared through the attrition of the years.

Then there is simply the old problem of carelessness. In going through hundreds or perhaps thousands of books, it is impossible to be alert to every possible clue. No doubt, books signed by famous people—their signatures all but illegible, perhaps (for a truly awesome illegibility, go to Dickens's signature)—odd facts about a book's production, outlandish ideas advanced in the text (no matter how outlandish, there will be collectors of precisely that sort of material), first references to important historical or political events . . . such clues go unwitnessed for years, even as the books that contain them are picked up, looked at, leafed through, and then tossed aside to be ignored until the next time.

You have to know everything; and in lieu of this, you have constantly to forgive yourself for your ignorance or inattention or carelessness. Happily, most of our errors pass without our knowing, for it is only the most boorish purchaser who will call your attention to some fact that you yourself should have detected, which fact would have justified your doubling or even tripling the price at which the book was actually offered.

Obversely, when you find a book signed by George Armstrong Custer or Nathaniel Hawthorne, and it is not accounted for in the price, buy it and keep your mouth shut. Or if you have to talk about it (as I am about to do), do so anonymously, and take something like credit for yourself (or gloat over the gratuitous fact of simply being lucky) without diminishing another.

The story I have to tell should not really embarrass the woman who sold me a certain book, for it is quite possible that she did not, physically, see the telling point. This was in a small-town bookstore in the South, and the book in question was a dictionary—obviously eighteenth century, but evidently missing the title page. The eighteenth-century calf binding was in good shape (a near miracle in this fact), and the text was very good. But no title page. So the book was priced at $12.00.

I stood for a long moment staring at the place where the title page should have been, but all this staring did not make it appear. And yet, there was something a little odd about the paste down. It didn't seem quite even. Perhaps the fly leaf was stuck to it. So I picked at the edge of the paper until it came loose, and lo, what opened up was not the fly leaf, but the title page itself, which read:

A

DICTIONARY

OF THE

ENGLISH LANGUAGE:

IN WHICH

The Words are Deduced from their Originals,

Explained in their Different Meanings,

AND

Authorized by the NAMES of the WRITERS in

whose Works they are found.

Abstracted from the Folio Edition,

by the Author

SAMUEL JOHNSON, A.M.

And so forth, further indicating that it is the third edition, "carefully revised," and published in Dublin in 1768. A Dublin piracy, no doubt; it is not listed in Courtney and Smith's *Bibliography* of Johnson, but the fact that it came out in 1768 is consistent with the date of the third edition's appearance, for it was first printed in London in 1765.

It is understandable that this particular dealer might have missed the title page, for it clings to the front pastedown cunningly and persistently. But it's possible she saw the red leather spine strip, which states simply, though not very clearly, *Johnson's Dictionary*. If she did in fact notice this and if she knew her bibliography, she would have known that this couldn't have been a first (which was published in two volumes); but she would have sighed over it, lamenting the ostensibly missing title page, and knowing that, since it was an eighteenth-century printing, it would have to be worth more than $12.00 if it were complete, no matter what edition or printing it was.

Missionaries of the Eternally Unspoken Word

Soon after the organization of the county of Meigs," Stillman C. Larkin wrote, in his *Pioneer History,* "a company of prominent citizens of Athens purchased lands of the Ohio Company's Purchase, situated as river bottom farms, above Old Town Creek." This land that Larkin speaks of was hilly, wild, and heavily timbered, and it was already sparsely settled by a tough and dogmatic breed of frontiersman.

The Athens County settlers of the 1820s, however, were evidently of a more refined sort; after all, this county bore the name of the crown of western civilization, whereas Meigs County had been named for Return J. Meigs, who, as a governor of the young frontier state was an estimable man, no doubt . . . but the county named for him had at this time shown little evidence of cultural aspiration.

What did these latter-day Athenians do with their newly acquired lands? Larkin tells us expansively: "Col. Shipman built a two-story hewed-log house, well finished, in which he had a storeroom for general merchandise. Mr. Ziba Lindley, Sr., put up a house of logs hewn on the inner side, with floors, doors, windows and partitions done by a regular 'house joiner'. Ziba Lindley, Jr. erected a two-story hewed-log house, well finished as to floors, doors, windows and bedroom partitions, a stone chimney, with open fireplaces to each story." Note the details: partitions done professionally by a "house joiner"; logs hewn *on the inner side;* a two-story log house whose stone chimney contained fire places *on both floors.* Such references imply a dark, severe, and occasionally violent existence against which humble refinements of this sort were noteworthy.

But the witness of the Athenians was not confined to matters of animal comfort and household embellishment. One of their cabins was converted into a schoolhouse, in which a Colonel Shipman also conducted religious services. On Sunday afternoons, these immigrants from the next county met to sing. They were excellent singers, according to Larkin, and carried "all the parts to time as correct as a military drill," with an effect that was evidently inspiring.

No doubt, these people were themselves inspired. And no doubt their inspiration was that of the missionary, a spirit whose fervors and zealous witnessings boiled throughout the populace of that time, erupting in strange and impetuous ways.

And yet, there are and have always been those who are impervious to the sweet influences of learning and deaf to the power of a correct and melodious music. Such, obviously, were the rude inhabitants of the wild hills above Old Town Creek. They were unmoved by the songs they heard. "The native population did not assimilate," Larkin sadly reported, "for they preferred the fiddle and such dances as suited their ideas of pleasure."

Through their teaching and the sweet controlled strains of their singing, the Athenians had hoped to convert their neighbors, Anglo-Saxon and Celtic backwoodsmen, not far different from themselves in their heritage, and inspire them to help create a more genteel and cultured society in the forest. But they were no more successful than the white man generally was with the Redman, whose dark and demonic soul, it was believed, could seldom nourish an alien growth of learning.

So eventually, exasperated and thoroughly discouraged, the Athenians relinquished their handsomely built log houses and returned to their own county. They left behind them a man named Bicknell to act as agent in selling and renting the land they had so foolishly and idealistically purchased. Bicknell thereby proved to be the only one among them who permanently settled down in this land of the wild turkey, deer, and fiddle. In fact, Bicknell married and raised a family, becoming one of the fathers of the new county.

But he always remembered that one brief flare of hope and purpose that had burst out in the hearts of the people from Athens. To the end of his days, he felt like something of an exile from that period of youthfulness and idealism. Larkin ends his story of the Athenian settlement with an austere reference to the unfortunate Bicknell: "He spoke often of his disappointment in the abandonment of the neighborhood by the Lindleys and Shipmans, as he had anticipated their good influences to bring about a better social environment."

Larkin's brief story holds a unique fascination for us. One can't help being sympathetic with the "Lindleys" and "Shipmans" in their zeal to reform and cultivate those backwoods fiddlers, who naturally and fittingly remain anonymous, since they were by vocation rejectors not only of polite music but of school learning, the Book, and the Word.

The conflict between these two human communities is elemental, and the full character of its premises is, like that of most human premises, inscrutable. That the conflict still continues in a myriad transformation is beyond question. "The Academic Establishment" is as insecure and ill established as any establishment might be. And, more particularly, those of us who teach the humanities look out upon a decreasingly hostile but increasingly indifferent world of fiddlers who will not sit in our schoolhouse and will not listen to our harmonies.

Today, the fiddle has been replaced by the electronic media. And in our sourest moments, we find ourselves in the posture of witnessing these invading hordes of younger and younger generations, fixed like heliotropic growths to the godlike glow of video games and the television set, upon which the mythic representations of our time are perpetuated.

Thus the fate of Ziba Lindley and Col. Shipman and their small group of cultural missionaries seems to prompt us to grasp for some powerful if ambiguous meaning that is never quite in reach. Cynicism and despair are not really justified, however, because for all its grandiose failures, the impulse toward art and learning has never been abandoned for long, and the ideals are as alive as ever, even though they are dressed in different styles of clothing and often seem to speak of entirely different matters.

But the essential point is this: some actions are secretly fulfilled somewhere in the shadow, this side of ostensible fulfillment. Some ideals exist only *as* ideals, which means that they will never be tangible, or fulfilled, any more than they will ever totally cease to be. Ideals are hybrids after all; and half of what they are is unreality. It is this share of unreality they possess that beguiles us into thinking they are possible—because the future is also an unreality;

and it is as if we can believe that ideals, simply by their being half unreal, might have one foot in the future.

It is not really this simple, to be sure; but nothing about ideals is simple, for they are very complex human facts. And if we are "beguiled," we are never really deceived or cheated, for the visions themselves, tantalizing and half-real, enlarge us. The emblem that occurs to me most often in this contest is the horseshoe, whose center of gravity is empty space. We are like that and, in our happier moments, embrace the fact, almost tangibly. There is no clearer model for our aspirations than this.

Therefore, it can be argued that those quixotic missionaries who journeyed forth from Athens into the wilderness so long ago were not defeated after all, even though their well-hewed cabins were all abandoned. The time they were there, carrying "all the parts to time as correct as a military drill" and trying to teach book learning to wild frontiersmen, was not really lost or wasted. Indeed, it is always hard to estimate the consequences of conviction. If you bear witness to something, how long can your voice be heard?

It was shortly after the Athenian experiment that Ambrose Bierce was born in Meigs County, at a settlement called "Horse Cave Creek." A passion for beauty and learning does not itself have to march as correctly as a military drill, nor does it have to permeate whole populations. The germ can exist and even flourish in strange and unlikely places, in strange and unlikely ways. It can even flower after decades of dormancy, in the writing of so passionate a misanthrope that he earned the sobriquet of "Bitter Bierce."

But even in Ambrose Bierce's relentlessly documented hatred for the vileness of humanity, the ambiguity of idealism is everywhere present. It is known by its absence, where the ideal always exists, a diapason to the world that is audible, real, and explicit. You can almost hear that beautiful and wistful singing today, after all these years.

As for Larkin's *Pioneer History of Meigs County*—which has inspired these ruminations upon time and learning—it was published in Columbus in 1908. On the flyleaf of my copy is written: "Crary Davis, February 21, 1921. Presented by Judge C. E. Peoples." Crary Davis was an attorney whose library I purchased many years ago, after his death. He lived in a big frame house in Middleport, which is in Meigs County and was named for the fact it is the halfway point between Pittsburgh and Cincinnati on the Ohio River.

I did not know Crary Davis, but by the evidence of his library, I would judge that he had learned and scholarly ideals. As for Judge Peoples, I know nothing. But I would assume he was a resident of Meigs County, as was Attorney Davis. Not to mention Col. Shipman, Ziba Lindley, and all those others who have somehow managed to perpetuate a faith in the human importance of such symbolic configurations as words, musical notes on a page, or a combination of both . . . of "cultural matters," in short, in a day when that expression could be written without quotation marks.

Adventures Following Old Trails

People often have difficulty understanding why anyone would have an interest in collecting the published journals and memoirs of early preachers in the Ohio valley, and I can think of no better explanation than inviting them to sample the testimony of these hardy, strong-voiced, cussedly pious circuit riders who spread the Gospel throughout the wilderness in the shadows of the Delaware, Wyandot, and Shawnee.

In the 1840s a preacher named Elder Levi Purviance (I hear his last name rhyme with "defiance") wrote a biographical sketch of another preacher named Reuben Dooly. Marvelous names, fitting together like segments of fate, as snug as cause and effect. This is history, and both men lived in and around some primitive version of Dayton, Ohio, as it then existed.

As traveling preachers, they knew the forests as Indians knew them, only instead of stalking in silence, these men sang hymns while they sat on their horses and rocked through the great darknesses of walnut, oak, and sycamore that separated the little frontier settlements. Levi Purviance knew the woods as he knew how to preach—something to use and make work; he was a Presbyterian and had little nonsense in his head, but an awful fear of God.

Reuben Dooly had been a tough and holy man, older and therefore, by strict Presbyterian standards, smarter than young Elder Levi. ($\pi\rho\epsilon\sigma\beta\acute{u}\tau\epsilon\rho o\varsigma$, itself, means "elder"; the root also appears in "presbyopia," the pathology of age-ridden vision.) But his gift with words could hardly have been greater, as revealed by Purviance's commentary on Dooly's Gospel labors during a time of high water:

In company with his brother-in-law, he attempted to pass over seven mile creek in a canoe; the stream was so strong and ran so rapidly, that it carried them over a milldam, and precipitated them into the flood beneath. Brother Dooly felt that the prospect was very fair for drowning. But he was not afraid to trust that God who had been his help in days past. The force of the current carried them to shallow water, and they made their escape, but Brother Dooly lost his hat. He pushed towards his appointments—an elderly lady gave him an old low crowned wool hat; he received it with thankfulness and went on to preach. At one of his appointments he met a good brother that gave him a good hat and took his old one. No man was more resolute than he was. "Whatsoever his hand found to do, he did it with his might." His heroic mind soared above discouragements.

I confess to finding this close to being a miracle of sturdy, good prose—antic and comical, too—and in the closing sentence I picture Dooly's mind wearing that good hat as it goes soaring over the dank weeds of despair. And the sentence that states, "Brother Dooly felt that the prospect was very fair for drowning," surely deserves a place somewhere among the glories of our language.

But lest we take too much mirth from the loss and subsequent trading of hats, we should remember how difficult and expensive the making of clothes was in those days, especially in the western regions where industry did not yet flourish, and people were scarce and as likely as not capable of being possessed by an awful ignorance, and could believe that unbaptized infants were eternally damned and thunder caused milk to sour in August.

And the truth is, I am glad that brother Dooly was not drowned. And I am pleased that he lived to make his way back into the world of hats. If he had not, Elder Levi Purviance could not have written what he did.

The company of a good writer quickens and brightens the mind, and Elder Levi Purviance was a good writer. His energy was such that he did well in ways he might not have recognized or been proud of. He took to the English sentence with an instinctive grace and vigor, and I would have liked to hear him preach. Speaking of another minister of his acquaintance, Nathan Worley, he wrote that, "Everything about the man seemed to preach," and later on commented that, "His general deportment in public and private life, was a volume of instruction to all his intimate acquaintances."

These words might well apply to Purviance, himself, and we are reminded of the truth that what people find in others to admire is part of what they themselves are. Possessed of a thoughtful and vivid mind, Levi Purviance saw these qualities when they were there to be seen in a brother preacher; emphatic and honest, he did not hesitate to give evidence of such traits in the elders he'd known and lived among. No occasion was too humble for his witnessing. Speaking of still another colleague, William Kinkade, he wrote:

> At one time he was preaching in a grove, a brother brought his family of children forward to do for them, after the custom of fathers. One little boy finding some objections in his mind to this ceremony; ran off, a short distance and climbed up a sapling, his father ordered him down; he swore, profanely, he would not come down. When brother Kinkade heard THAT, he said, "I will not baptize that one."

Well, I probably wouldn't have, either; and I don't think such a stand would be found necessarily supportive of the doctrine of Infant Damnation, but it is surely not inconsistent with it.

Elder Kinkade was no coward, nor was he shy. He "had something of poetical genius," Levi Purviance says, "but he had no tune, he could not sing or even imitate singing; yet he was resolute to try and try again."

There is style in this utterance, as in so many others from his pen. Elder Levi's meaning is clear when he says that Brother Kinkade "had no tune"; we have all known folks of this sort; but when he goes on to say, "he could not sing or even imitate singing," what, exactly, can he mean? How do you *imitate* singing? Are we to believe that Brother Kinkade couldn't silently move his lips as if singing the words of a hymn? Surely, he could do this. What, then, can "imitate singing" refer to?

I think he means that Brother Kinkade was not simply a man who could not carry a tune, but a man who couldn't even come *near* singing a tune. There must be important differentiations in the class of hitting the wrong note in singing. I had never thought of this before, but evidently Elder Kinkade was so gifted in this way that he could go through an entire chorus without once, even by chance, landing on the right note. He was evidently so far off the mark that his efforts were capable of inspiring awe in those who listened.

When confronted with an anecdote like this, you have trouble knowing where self-ignorance ends and courage begins. Did Kinkade *think* he was singing? We'll never know; Purviance's testimony does not reach this far. Was Kinkade aware that he was missing the tune, but simply threw himself onto the Lord's mercy and just yelled away at whatever hymn lay before him? Again, silence. Also darkness.

Even more obviously unsuited for the ministry was young Elder Thomas Adams, for while Kinkade was unfitted to sing, he could at least preach well; but Adams, it appears, started in preaching without being able even to *talk* coherently.

> He persevered through difficulties that an irresolute mind would never have overcome. His opportunity for improvement had been by no means good. His manner of address was awkward, and his language imperfect; and he spoke just as fast as his tongue could possibly run; upon the whole, he had nothing to recommend him but his upright deportment and honest zeal. It was a tax upon any person of taste, to listen to him. Under these circumstances he met with very little encouragement from his brethren, particularly preachers; some of them treated him with neglect and contempt, but others believing him to be an honest and devout young man, endeavored to bear him up.

What business did a babbler like this have in trying to preach? He must have been badly afflicted, for Purviance states that Elder George Shidler once told him that "he had received more persecution, for encouraging Brother Thomas Adams, than he ever had from any other quarter in his life. The people were offended at him," Brother Shidler continues, "because he would take him [Adams] with him and encourage him to speak."

Eventually, Brother Shidler was vindicated, for Adams was utterly transformed from that passionately ignorant and incoherent youth into a scholarly and eloquent preacher—one of the greatest Levi Purviance had ever known. "We find not that boy laboring under almost every embarrassment, imaginable," he wrote, after which he exhorts as follows: "Reader, in your imagination you may travel as far to the reverse as you reasonably can, and you will not leave him in the rear."

These little samples of Levi Purviance's style are marvelous, in their way; but then, everything this old preacher wrote is illuminated by the same spirit.

What is even more remarkable is that the passages quoted above are all from the same book, and not even from the main portion of it. The book itself is titled:

THE
BIOGRAPHY OF
ELDER DAVID PURVIANCE,
with his memoirs: containing his views on Baptism, the
Divinity of Christ, and the Atonement.

WRITTEN BY HIMSELF:

WITH AN APPENDIX:
GIVING
BIOGRAPHICAL SKETCHES
OF
Elders John Hardy, Reuben Dooly, William Dye,
Thos. Kyle, George Shidler, William Kinkade,
Thomas Adams, Samuel Kyle, and Nathan Worley.
TOGETHER WITH A HISTORICAL SKETCH OF THE
GREAT KENTUCKY REVIVAL.

By Elder Levi Purviance.

DAYTON.
Published for the Author by B. F. & G. W. Ells

1848

The title page suggests that this is in effect an autobiography, but
the phrase "written by himself" is somewhat ambiguous. Elder
David Purviance is consistently referred to in the third person, and
one gets the impression that this is David's son, Levi, writing about
his father.

But I suspect the father had a hand in the whole business, for he
was alive at the time it was written, and the overtly autobiographi-
cal part does not have the flair for anecdote and the sense of character that illuminate the short biographical sketches at the end. Stylistically, the prose is nearer to what one would expect of the local
Rotary Club president than of Herodotus.

Therefore, one must conclude that, in this case, the child really *is*
father to the man, for Levi is a vastly superior writer. And it is in
these biographical sketches bringing up the rear that one can sense
the genius of old preachers' accounts. The father's biography is an
act of *pietas,* and no doubt estimable in intent; but if you want to
savor the gnarled syntax and blunt, homely diction of frontier life,

you will have to go to the end pieces—conceived as afterthoughts, perhaps, but with more life on a single page than you can find in whole chapters of the main body of the work.

The faults and sins of omission in the main portion of this book represent the major blight upon the genre: too many pioneer preachers spent their energies and whatever talent they might have had upon proving how pious they were and how urgent it was for their flock and readers to get right with God. They were drunk on holiness, or at least the appearance of holiness, and the theological and religious themes they play tend to be of one note, and that a shrill one.

Of course, death and sickness were more a part of frontier life than we can easily believe. It isn't just that everybody died in those days, but a lot of them died early. Most of Levi Purviance's biographical notes are brief for one reason only: his subjects died young. William Dyer was typical. Of him, Purviance wrote:

> He was a young man of exemplary character, and very promising. His appearance was grave and interesting. He bid fair to be a very popular and useful Preacher. But Oh! how uncertain are all human calculations. The messenger of death, like an unexpected visitor, came at a time not looked for, and blasted the prospects of his friends and the hopes of the church, and he was cut down in the bloom of his days, and prime of life. Leaving an affectionate wife, and a few small children to mourn their loss. Whilst the Church felt sensibly the stroke, and lamented the disappointment. His death was occasioned by a severe cold, that terminated in a fever. His funeral discourse was preached by Elder Kyle.

This sorrowful event does not lend itself to Levi Purviance's more vigorous expressions, but there is one item of interest in the passage quoted above. It is stated that Dyer's "appearance was grave and interesting." This is an interesting, though hardly grave, conjunction. Think of the obligatory smile in modern portraits, even snapshots (if your image isn't smiling, there's likely something wrong with you) and contrast the cheerfulness we are meant to project with that evangelical gravity. There were obviously people in the frontier West of that day who could appreciate a jesting curate; and yet gravity was the tune they were meant to dance to. Contrast this with today's minister, who, if he "doesn't have a sense of humor" (possessed as tangibly as a winning smile, a dimple, a good voice, and an ability to speak clearly and fashionably upon topics of concern in today's society), is in danger of being held in contempt, if not actually being stigmatized as un-Christian.

However, the lugubriousness and relentlessly pietistic tone of many old journals are enough to turn readers away after the briefest sampling, and this is a pity, as the entries from Levi Purviance should demonstrate. Most who have read in this specialized literature feel the frustration of reading an account that should reflect some of the richness and energy of the world without, but is instead stultifying in its dull and undeviating insistence upon a pale and insubstantial holiness.

Ernest J. Wessen, the great Americana book dealer, commented upon this in a letter to Mrs. Norah Wood, one of his book scouts. His letter begins:

Dear Mrs. Wood:

"They were so intent scanning the skies in search of a sign from Heaven; that they failed to note God's handiwork; which they trod beneath their dirty feet."

I wrote it years ago, and it has since been quoted in *Publisher's Week* [sic]; *Library Quarterly* and other bookmen's sheets. It was written with particular reference to the published memoirs of pioneer preachers and missionaries. So many of them prove to be utterly worthless; while they could have lived, as their writers' hoped, had they only recorded the passing scene.

Your George Wilson is about the worst I have ever seen . . . for he really muffed a bet. He was in the same vicinity . . . in close proximity to Lincoln, on one occasion. Had he only devoted a paragraph, even a single line . . . , but no!, he must record his thoughts and, like the rest, did so with no realization that these were teachings he had absorbed which, had he put them into practice, would have made his life worthwhile. I'm so sorry that his record is worthless, and I am having to return it.

Well, it's a shame that Wessen couldn't have read Levi Purviance's short biographies at the end of David Purviance's "biography"—the first part is almost dull enough to stand with George Wilson's account, but these brief notes at the end are marvelous, in their way, and worthy of the attention of anyone who savors the genius of the English language.

To speak of the "roughness of frontier life" is so commonplace that there seems to be little cause to contemplate its truth. And yet, reading in such literature as I have been celebrating will make that roughness familiar and real, possessed of details and documented by episodes that should be enough to bring the commonplace of a distant and alien time alive.

The fact is, many of these people who settled the midwestern woodlands during and after the Indian wars lived a brutish existence. Even a half-civilized preacher riding circuit among them would likely show forth as a beacon—not just of decent piety—but of sophistication, sensitivity, and *politesse*. And yet often, simply in order to communicate (as we would say today), a preacher had to speak the language of the frontier—which is to say, he had to prove himself physically, which is to say further, show he was able to "take it and dish it out."

Probably the heavyweight champion communicator of these times was "Billy Cravens," whose piety and prowess were the subject of the Rev. J. B. Wakeley's *The Bold Frontier Preacher: A Portraiture of Rev. William Cravens, of Virginia* (Cincinnati, 1869). This little 119-page book is filled with accounts of Cravens's pugilistic and evangelical success (testified by a variety of witnesses) over the years.

Billy Cravens was a physical prodigy, standing six feet tall, weighing 275 pounds, "with every limb well proportioned and every muscle disciplined up to the fullest vital force." (I take that to mean he was, in spite of his great weight, fully coordinated and without fat. And all this without steroids!)

Wakeley's little book abounds in anecdote. Classically, Cravens began life as a boistrous whiskey-drinking ruffian. A local champion once came to him, saying he had heard that Cravens was the best fighter in three counties, goading him until Cravens finally picked him up and "threw him almost a rod" over a fence. When his bruised and bewildered antagonist was finally able to speak coherently, he humbly admitted defeat, and then asked Cravens if he would kindly throw his horse over the fence after him, so he could make his way back home.

The riotous phase of Cravens's life ended when he got religion, sometime near the end of the eighteenth century. From that time on, he was a Methodist whose sworn enemies were liquor and slavery. Also from that time, he was blind in one eye, having lost the other from a chip of stone that flew up from his hammer while he was working as a stone mason.

Wakeley tells us that Cravens was not the only one-eyed preacher of the time: he cites Thomas Webb, "one of the founders of Western Methodism," along with Gideon Ousley, "Ireland's greatest missionary the great battle ax against Popery," and a Welsh orator with the marvelous name of Christmas Evans. Maybe one eye is better than two when it comes to fervid witnessing and the hardships of the frontier; just as two eyes are better for assemblies and dialectic, with the finicky perspectives available to binocular vision.

Having become a man of cloth did not relieve Billy Cravens from the challenges of lesser men. Like the gun fighters two generations later (especially as pictured in the media four generations after *that*), Billy Cravens could not lay down his guns.

That is to say, just about every local tough who gazed upon his amazing physique was tempted to measure himself against such mightiness. Cravens must have appeared to them as a living, walking, human carnival bell to be rung by a mighty stroke of a mallet . . . or perhaps a legendary unridable horse, or some other absolute of virile attainment.

Those who challenged Brother Cravens were a heterogeneous lot, and the occasions of their assaults upon him were various: all they had in common was that they were all quickly, easily, ignominiously defeated. One of the most colorful was a blacksmith in Virginia, who—Wakeley tells us—"was a great enemy of the Methodists, and especially Methodist preachers." Wakeley continued:

It was his practice to whip every one that came on to the circuit. Several were whipped severely by the belligerent blacksmith. Mr. Cravens heard of him, and had an appointment on the circuit, and was under the necessity of passing the dreaded blacksmith's shop. As he approached it the smith knew him by his dress, and coming out from the shop seized the reins of Mr. Cravens' horse and inquired "if he was a Methodist minister?" He answered "Yes." The blacksmith, who had a brawny arm, told him he "whipped every Methodist minister that passed his shop, and he must prepare for a licking." "Come on," said Mr. Cravens, "if I must take it." The blacksmith made several passes at Mr. Cravens, which he parried off. He then dismounted from his horse, seized the blacksmith, who was an infant in his arms, threw him upon his back, placed his knees on his stomach, and sung one of his favorite hymns. Holding him down with his great weight, the man was very uncomfortable, and cried out, "Lord have mercy on me." "Amen," said Cravens; "that is a good prayer; say it again." He then made him repeat the Lord's prayer after him, and would not let him up till he had promised never to interfere with another Methodist preacher. It is said, from that circumstance, the blacksmith was awakened and converted, and became a very useful member of the church.

Episodes like this are touched with the magic simplicity of folk and fairy tales. And while they are the main theme of Billy Cravens's adventures, they do not show him fully. He could evidently be eloquent, in his way, and Wakeley makes clear that he could best an unwashed murmur of infidels by logic as well as by fist. He could also resort to sarcasm when taunted, and addressed his bellicose and uncouth antagonists as "my honeys" before destroying them in argument.

As for the character of those arguments, they do not show a wit that is commensurate with Brother Cravens's physical authority, but they are adequate. When a man argued in defense of what we would call "social drinking," Cravens repudiated him by saying that social drinking was no more different from drunkenness than pigs from hogs. Wakeley explains the point to the reader by stating that just as pigs grow into hogs, so do social drinkers become drunkards.

Preacher Cravens was a mighty man, beyond doubt. And Wakeley's account makes lively reading. Perhaps its finest moment passes so quickly it could almost be lost: while addressing a large and hostile crowd, Cravens finished and prepared to depart. Darkness had fallen, and he asked one of those present to hold a torch on the side of his missing eye, while he made his way through the throng.

Wakeley judiciously avoids giving emphasis to this small fact, but the inference is there waiting: Brother Cravens was not afraid of anything in this world, so long as he could see it. As for things invisible, he was both wary and pious, in spite of his massive strength and cool head. It was what he couldn't see out of his blinded eye that occupied his life and sent him hither and yon in the wilderness, prompted by the call in his heart. Wakeley puts the matter quaintly: "Mr. Cravens often went from impressions," he wrote. Which seems about as good a motive as any, when viewed from the perspective afforded by two eyes over one and a half centuries.

What Should We Do with the Past?

I often brood over this question. How should we relate to it? How should we file it away? What objects will we retain as emissaries of past years in the chaos and evolution of the present? What will such symbolic forms mean for us? How will some be adapted (as in the restoration or renovation of antique furniture) to our current judgments of grace and beauty? How can the past be effectively translated into our own immediate and recognizable forms, for our living benefit? How can the past prove relevant? What kind of house cleaning goes on in our minds (where, presumably, the past accumulates) when we don't even know it? What are the uses of the past?

These are some of the questions that cluster around that central one. As problems, I like them. They are not urgent, therefore they can really be worked over; they don't demand immediate, specific action; they are open, impractical, intellectual; they challenge the free play of the imagination; they seem whimsical and gratuitous.

And yet, I think the central question of what to do with the past is important. I suspect it might be sneaky, insidious, universal. If the term were not so badly overused, I would call it "a critical question." Not, of course, critical in the sense that our decisions regarding energy inventories, environmental pollution, racism, international financial anarchy, unemployment, terrorism, and inflation are critical (for these do demand specific actions guided by forethought and wisdom at the cost, often, of very tangible penalties), but critical in the sense that our constant, mostly habitual (and therefore unconsidered) disposal and retention of the past have a great deal to do with the shape, color, and temper of our lives.

91

BOOKING IN THE HEARTLAND

It is said that our bodies are, not what we eat, but what our kidneys choose to retain; similarly, our sense of life, which is to say the box we live in, is constructed basically of those elements of the past which our minds, like mnemonic sorting organs, choose to retain. Therefore, the question of what to do with the past may prove ultimately to be more profoundly critical than those obviously more urgent concerns. Because of their revolutionary premise, socialist countries have had to face this problem in particularly vivid ways: the Russians in the "Cult of the Personality" attacks in their de-Stalinization drive, and the Chinese in their early revolutionary attacks upon Confucius and the Confucian culture and tradition.

Try asking a politician: "Senator, what do you think we should do with the past?" After his initial reconnaissance of the unfamiliar terrain behind this question, he might just possibly (if he senses enough public concern) form a committee to study the issue. Who knows, he might be visited by the notion that the dead have a vote. Come to think of it, maybe they do.

Which wild surmise brings us almost squarely back to that initial question that began as my private whimsy, but is trying to become a fully articulated, public idea. Let us think about it.

If the past were nothing but mere tracings of our passage through time, deposited like vanishing blips on a radar screen, there would be no problem at all. We would have no memory, no consistency, no logic, no identity, no hang-ups, no happiness in any conceivable human sense.

But the past is stubborn, tenacious—the uninvited house ghost that stays for dinner. As the Faulkner character says: "The Past isn't dead; it isn't even past." And indeed the past is precisely that which isn't lost. That which is lost is . . . well, lost, and we can't very well conceive of it at all, let alone analyze and pass judgment on it.

The haunting question always returns: What do we decide, either tacitly or overtly, to retain, and what to forget? And in what ways are we making decisions, not just tacitly, but so casually and essentially that we are not even aware, at one remove, of our negligence to consider what we are about . . . are not even near enough awareness to be prepared to understand, when we are challenged, how permeant and ubiquitous our dealing with the past is, and how profoundly unaware we are of this fact?

Of course, we do have familiar ways to cope with the past. Planned obsolescence is one. Seeming to deny or obviate the past, in the sense that automobiles are constructed to last ten years, and buildings for only thirty, planned obsolescence is in reality a method for taming the past. Bringing it into control, predictability. If you design a restaurant with the premise that its economic life will be thirty years (mortgage loans, depreciation schedules, capital investment tax credits, etc., will figure in this hypothesis), you are saying something about social time and a predicted trajectory of change that, as a self-fulfilling prophecy, tends to become a scenario. Which means, of course, that you are saying something about the past . . . not merely as the base upon which you extrapolate schedules of obsolescence, but as a medium in which things take place, happen, last on.

There are more tangible examples. Used car businesses, garage sales, realty companies, law offices, court rooms, dry cleaning establishments, and junk stores are all places committed in one way or another to dealing with the past.

But nowhere, and in no way, is the past processed so vividly and colorfully and directly as in the familiar auction of household goods. Surely, this fact helps explain the almost hypnotic appeal of these Saturday morning rituals for so many people. Typically, such an auction is for the settling of an estate "of one deceased." And when crowds mill about, nuzzling china, palpating the springs of a tired old sofa, holding glassware up in the sunlight (I visualize this as a country auction), they may seem like the ugliest and motliest lot of scavengers ever to participate in the last ritual of someone's life (for that person's death was only his penultimate act). And when the auctioneer stands up on the back porch or a table or wheelbarrow, and all that miscellany of people fix their gaze upon him, awaiting the start of his chant . . . why, well might you ask if ever a brood of buzzards or a murder of crows looked more portentous and unkind as they gazed upon a corpse.

And yet, scavengers we are not (for I am among them, standing in back, where I can't see the defects in the things I'll probably bid on). No, we are not unkind or unfeeling in our standing there, waiting for the first notes of the auctioneer's *recitativo*. Rather, we are clerics in the service of property, and celebrants in the ritual processing and dispersal of the past.

Do you think there is something shameful in our being there, bidding mere dollars for the right to possess the crazy quilt that old Mrs. Duncan loved and labored upon for so many years, or the needlepoint that Mrs. Walker ruined her eyes over? Not at all. We are perpetuating the worth of things once lived with and, at best, cherished. We are participating in one last gesture of appreciation.

If such noble and romantic ideas are not always present in the minds of bidders, it doesn't matter. After all, we seldom know what we are about or why we are doing a particular thing, anyway. And if our unacknowledged motives are usually found, under close scrutiny, to be far shabbier than we could have guessed, why can't they at least sometimes be a little better than we imagined?

But for the most dogged cynic, there might be only one resort in his analysis of the moral character of an auction of household goods: What, really, is the alternative to their disposal in this way? It just might be that old Mrs. Duncan and Mrs. Walker have never in their whole lives been the cause of so much pleasure and excitement at one time. And that goes for their predeceased husbands, too.

I suppose it's no secret by now. I love country auctions. I like the sight of cars lined up along a dirt road, a crowd of people milling about old oak dressers and hay rakes and trestle tables, and digging their hands in sagging cardboard boxes of sheet music from the early 1900s, postcards, toy soldiers, button collections, and old clothes. I like the smell of freshly made coffee and beef barbecue (Sloppy Joes), and the tinkle of wind chimes from the breezeway in back, and the loud, gravelly voices of old farmers as they talk about politics and the weather, and their lumpy old wives who, with a prim tightening of lips, pick up a glass pitcher or salad bowl and scrutinize it in a long, unblinking stare. Yes, these are my people, and I know them.

However, my fascination is fed by more than this babble of relics and their ritual dispersal; it is fed even more richly, on lucky days, by the particular things I bring away from the auction. And I am there primarily to find old books, to bid on them, to buy them.

Not all the books I get bear vivid testimony to the historical past, for always part of the adventure consists in the unpredictability of what you will find. It is of the nature of books that their heterogeneity is greater than that of the world of historical fact. No matter how bizarre a thing or notion is, it may be represented in a book; but the ghosts that dwell in books far outnumber the earthly kind, for books contain marching windmills, golden fleece, spiders that can spell, and talking trees. So whenever you hear someone say, "Truth is stranger than fiction," you should realize that the speaker of such cant does not know his fiction; which in this context means, he does not know the facts. And that's the truth.

But back to the subject, which is unpredictability. I never know what I will find in a box of books at an auction. I have a pretty good idea, it is true: it will be four smudged and tattered *Methodist Hymnals,* one copy of *The Man Nobody Knows,* by Bruce Barton, and *I Have Four Apples,* by Josephine Lawrence. Also, there will be a copy of *The Prisoner of Zenda,* by Anthony Hope, only the cover and title page will be missing, so it will require a brief fit of fondling for me to identify it.

Wait. This is predictable, again, but I am really expecting the unexpected. Today, in this context, at this auction, I'm looking for those other books. I am looking for messages from the past, in the form of local and county histories, biographies of old-time preachers, soldiers, and politicians, reports of historical societies, and so forth. Such books as these are in the likely-unlikely class—a class that is bordered on one side by the clearly impossible (I have never found a first edition of Swift or Fielding at a farm auction in Hocking County) and on the other by the virtually predestined (*I Have Four Apples,* etc.).

Constrained only by their astronomically rising prices, news of which occasionally penetrates as far as auctions in Pennsville and Shade, I have gotten, throughout the years, a lot of likely-unlikely, or common-rare Americana. Such books are almost always interesting, even when they are poorly written (which they often are); and they are at best downright fascinating for the impressions, both intended and accidental, they provide of our past.

I have been gathering these impressions for years, *pari passu* with my collecting Americana, and I have arrived at certain conclusions, the gist of which is rather sobering for those of us who are descendants of the "native sons" who settled the land and "carved the frontier out of the wilderness" . . . and, incidentally, went on to write books in which they created the foregoing clichés.

The conclusion, I think, is inescapable: those of us who are of "old American stock" are, unanimously and without exception, descended from as spectacular a bunch of crazies as ever inhabited the earth.

At first, their lunacy is not apparent. The reason is that one of the ways in which we use the past is to institutionalize it in particular forms (statues, national holidays, historical shrines, oratory, media references, etc.). We do this for various reasons, the most obvious being to help define ourselves, to preserve a sense of continuity (this is an enlarged cultural need similar to the individual's needs to have a memory at the cost of not having a mind and thereby not being oneself), and finally to help stabilize the present, the society around us. All of these motives are related, of course; but the last is the most challengeable in terms of whatever we might mean by such words as "justice" or "the good life."

These are some of things we have, in the past, done with the past, some of the ways we have tried to cope with it. Naturally, by institutionalizing the past, we warp it, change it for our own often-concealed and/or misunderstood needs. We also, by the ceremonial repetition of its symbols, familiarize it, since repetition induces familiarity, and through it, one sort of comprehension.

When we institutionalize real live human beings (or at least those who were once real and live), we translate them, abstract them, stereotype them. Often, we canonize them. You could give serious and prolonged study to a statue of Abraham Lincoln and never guess, from it alone, that its subject was a man who loved tricky argumentation, brooded about death, and enjoyed naughty jokes. But that's all right: the statue is one way in which we use the past, and this way is perfectly defensible. But it isn't the whole truth. It isn't even a major portion.

Lincoln probably wasn't as crazy as the people around him, which makes him sort of . . . crazy, I guess. But look at photographs of his contemporaries. Pick any group of pictures, or choose at random. Study those visages well. Notice the jolly, laughing faces, the relaxed stances of the men, the warmth of expression of the women. Notice the generosity and openness delineated on their faces.

No, you'll see Lincoln's statue sneeze before you see humanity as we know it, let alone anything like warmth or happiness creep into those dark and cold photographs. But then, people were still in those days a little intimidated by the camera, which is a rather diabolical instrument, come to think about it. And then, people—especially in the Midwest and on the frontier—were also cursed by a grim, repressive Calvinism, and the blighting fetishes of social formality.

Also, considering deaths from typhoid, malaria, pneumonia, childbed fever . . . and a multitude of other diseases and infections that made their lifespan pathetically short by modern standards, maybe we can understand something of the reason for all those dour faces. In *Main Travelled Roads,* Hamlin Garland remarks that, throughout all his childhood in Wisconsin, he could hardly ever remember hearing a song that was happy. And in a marvelously worded comment, the historian Henry Howe says of Noah Webster, "I do not remember to have ever seen him smile. He was a too-much pre-occupied man for frivolity, bearing, as he did, the entire weight of the English tongue on his shoulders."

Still, we can surely understand this: as a man of dignity, of importance, of substance, the old lexicographer couldn't afford to be seen laughing or telling jokes or doing the hokey pokey. Who, even today, would trust a frolicsome maker of dictionaries?

But it's pretty safe to say that a lot of these people were generally devoid of self-irony, and in this sense, humorless. At least, when they had their photographs taken. Can you visualize General Winfield Scott in bathing trunks, mugging for the camera?

There was a strong tradition of popular humor, of course, but it was generally pretty crude. The comic genius of Mark Twain (and to a lesser extent, that of the fabulous or legendary Lincoln) is no more handsomely framed than against the drab background of his contemporaries' attempts to be funny. Consider that a large proportion of the popular jokes of this period had to do with Irishmen (Paddy) or blacks (Mose), whose behavior goes awry over some excessively literal response to a word. In short, the jokes turned on half-witted puns, and if they are any indication of the lighter side of life in those days, it's no wonder that all those faces in early photographs are so grim.

But this isn't quite right, either. The more information you gather, the more you have to keep hedging, footnoting, butting, how-evering, and neverthelessing. (Maybe the proud ignoramus is right, and it's better not even to start accumulating facts: why not keep things simple?)

Insofar as we can say they had no sense of humor (in our by-now-famous modern sense of that word), we must nevertheless protest that this isn't the same as saying they didn't manage to be humorous in themselves. Quite the contrary. When I referred to them as a "spectacular bunch of crazies," I was not implying, as indeed their photographs might pretty much unanimously suggest, that they suffered from advanced melancholia or catatonic paralysis or religious hysteria. The fact is (as we know from a close attention to all those books purchased at auctions), those photographs lie. And they don't just lie: they lie stupendously, superbly, incredibly. Those photographs show the people of those days pretending to be sober and venerable and dignified and stuffy and safe. And this pretense turns out to be the biggest gasser of all, because those people were really Parson Weems and Ned Buntline in disguise. Not to mention the James Brothers (Frank and Jesse, of course), Bozo the Clown, the Katzenjammer Kids, Orphan Annie, Margaret Fuller, and Bonnie and Clyde. All of them, every one.

I think my first inkling came years ago when I read about a young soldier in the Revolutionary War who was killed trying to catch a British cannonball as it came bouncing toward him. Curious? Well, you'd certainly think so. However, the account went on, this was not an isolated case. In fact, there were several deaths of this sort, and officers were forced to caution their men that those sizzling grounders couldn't be stopped by the best glove man in the business, because they were coming about twice as fast as they appeared to be moving, partly because they were a lot bigger than they looked; also they were made of cast iron and lead, which meant they weighed twenty or thirty or forty pounds, and would zip right through your cupped hand and smash your face right back into your occiput.

It is something of a shock to learn that such reckless boys were part of that sober and heroic army now apotheosized by the DAR. Why, these lads belonged to that ancient and venerable brotherhood of fools, which includes just about any boy who ever was or will be worth a damn. It includes poor drunk Elpenor falling off Circe's roof and breaking his neck, as well as Sir Francis Bacon (a curious old boy if there ever was one) packing a dead rooster with snow, thereby catching his own death of cold; it includes Archimedes drawing geometric figures in the sand, right under the shadow of that uptight Roman soldier's upright sword.

Is it possible that the founders of this nation were capable of playing? Even foolishness? Evidently, they were, indeed. And if the records are correct (which they just about have to be, they are so consistent in their revelation of traits their authors had little wish to emphasize), never have there been generations of men more impetuous, impulsive, exuberant, and irrational than these who "founded and built this nation." Trying to catch bounding cannonballs doesn't even begin to tell the story!

In short, most of them were mostly childlike, most of the time. Which is natural, perhaps, when you consider that the average life span was just out of teeny-bopper range. The gauntlet of deadly diseases I referred to earlier took its toll. But there was also the high incidence of drownings, death by fire, murder, and various accidental casualties. We think of the highway death toll as a modern innovation, but if valid statistics were available, the death rate per passenger mile of a hundred years ago would surely prove higher than today's. Traveling by stagecoach, for example, was a hazardous risk, especially in the Old West, when extra customers were forced to "ride" on the outside, as celebrated by the following dirge:

> Weep, Stranger, for a father spilled
> From a stagecoach, and thereby killed;
> By name, Bill Sykes, a maker of sassengers,
> Slain with three other outside passengers.

Therefore, considering all those gaudy exits from life, you were either old enough to be dignified, gouty, wary, and possessed of enough money to have your photograph taken, or you were still an adolescent, and probably acted like one.

But no, it is more than this. There was a qualitative difference. We try to understand the larger and more complex mysteries that surround us by imposing a familiar grid upon them. We visualize the universe as an awesomely expanded human being, and the stars as campfires. Or we conceive of light and sound as "waves," and electricity as a "current," because these more mysterious phenomena somewhat resemble the behavior of water.

Similarly, we project upon the flow of history the familiar patterns of our individual lives; thus it is that we think of our ancestors as fathers, forefathers, founding fathers, and so on. We identify the childhood of the race or country with our own childhood, when we were sustained and nourished in the comfort of parents who were obviously omnipotent, benign, and wise. In fact, excepting benignity, their early images last on in our memories a little like old daguerreotypes.

However, this particular grid is warped. Insofar as history is accumulative, each of us is older than his father, in the sense that he is living later in time, and is thereby participating in some of the consequences of his father's acts. Our filial vantage point is such that we can at least theoretically sit in judgment upon our father's acts in a way that he could never sit in judgment upon ours. We can see how the things he did and intended "turned out." We have, if not the truth, at least another perspective into the premises and passions of the generation in which he lived. In a cultural sense, we are all older than our fathers, and more sophisticated. Mankind— ourselves—has never been as old as it is today.

Because of the greater intimacy of our dependence upon our own fathers, the idea of their innocence is a little more difficult to accept than its larger, historical version. We may not be able to realize fully that the man who first taught us how to hold a baseball bat or fly rod simply did not have the opportunity to understand some of the things we take very much for granted, and have assimilated into our everyday attitudes and behavior; but when we look at old photographs of Civil War soldiers, we can hardly miss the fact that most of those boys were young and innocent almost beyond belief. They were adolescents, most of them, and many did not live long enough to become anything else, even supposing that they could have somehow transcended the world they lived in and achieved a mature perspective in any modern sense of the word.

This does not mean we have any right to be patronizing toward them. Of course not. History isn't all that incremental. There aren't many ways in which we can claim to be a "century smarter" than Darwin or the young Henry James, no matter how much has transpired in those hundred years. Even though the written records of our period (say of the last fifty years) just might possibly be greater than those of all other historical periods combined, who could possibly guess their plenary meaning?

No, in this context, the point is that, quite apart from our too ready willingness to sentimentalize about the past, or to luxuriate in the relaxing mind rubs of nostalgia . . . the point is that, beyond all those gloomy photos and religious cant, the majority of our forefathers behaved like children. They were impetuous, frantic, exuberant, thoughtless, insensitive, maudlin, reckless, imprudent, wild, and virtually devoid of sobriety. They were erratic, willful, crazy. They were, alas, pretty much like us. They didn't think. At least most of them—from senators to mule skinners—didn't. In contrast to the popular image of the cold and careful frontiersman, consider the reality of whole ragged populations boiling westward, forgetting powder horns, grandmothers, salt, pet cats, and children. Their motto was, "I didn't know it was loaded."

Lorenzo Dow, the famous traveling preacher, journeyed down the Ohio River in the heyday of the flatboat, and marveled at the number of red-shirted corpses floating in the water. Their red shirts signified that they were riverboat men, and one would think that enough of them could swim that their corpses wouldn't be all that plentiful. *One* would think, but obviously none of them hardly ever did.

Everything was a spectacle to these people—churches, dog fights, politicians, homeopathic surgeons, revivals, courtrooms, Fourth of July parades, and cholera scares. People were passionately litigious, fond of any contest, providing they could watch it or talk about it or bet upon it. Every village had its horse races, men races, and cock fights. Steamboats raced up and down the Ohio and Mississippi, and the safety valves were often wedged open with a block of wood, so that an occasional explosion, featuring flying bodies amid the debris, would liven things up.

There was an element of hysteria in all this, of course. And that's the point, or part of it . . . for the point becomes more and more commodious under scrutiny. Having survived their first winter, a Plymouth Bay settler said, "Praise God, half of us are still alive!" This attitude is the precise opposite of that legendary utterance of a Pennsylvania Dutch farmer, who—having lost one of his six pigs—lamented: "I've lost all my litter but five!"

If a bee hive or bear was seen high up in a tree, the result was splendidly foreordained: the tree would be chopped down, right then and there, even if buttermilk was needed for the dying preacher. And then the fun would begin. In fact, if he heard the commotion, the expiring preacher, like dead Finnegan in another energetic tradition, might conceivably climb out from under the covers and take off through the woods after the spooked bear or swirling hive. But he would return in time to utter his deathbed utterance for the edification of family and flock, and then likely as not die according to the prescribed way.

There is a careless and exuberant spirit observable even in their cruelties. At a student protest at the University of Virginia (where gentlemanly behavior has always been encouraged), a professor tried to caution the lads before him, and was shot dead for his efforts. I suspect there was little malice in the act, but the distinction is surely academic.

In Bryan, Ohio, a fence around the courthouse square was torn down by an angry mob, intent on seeing a hanging. The victim in this case was not Sile Doty—although Sile was a resident of this area much of his life, and was eminently deserving of the honor, according to every existing law. During his forty-year binge of happy-go-lucky marauding, "Old Sile the Horse Thief" probably stole more than Jesse James did, but he never had a good press agent and he lacked a gift for the grandiose coup.

Sile Doty never repented; and when he was old and broke, he said, "Not even the certainty of being hanged would have prevented me for one moment from taking something I wanted." A lot of scoundrels can be appreciated for their colorful ways and melodramatic accomplishments, providing they are far enough away in time or space; but apparently old Sile had a certain cantankerous streak of the likable in his make-up he could never quite quench, for upon his release from one of his prison terms, both he and the warden wept.

And speaking of crying, there was the Reverend Jesse Lee, a century before, who, when he was conscripted to fight the British in the War for Independence, swore that he would not carry arms. His commanding officer tried in vain to change his mind; but he didn't know the strength of conviction in the man he confronted. Finally, Jesse Lee began to preach and pray to the men about him, right there at muster, and before long all about him were weeping openly—officers, men, and maybe even a passing dog or mule. By God, they had some real preachers in those days! Just consider what might have happened if the Rev. Lee and Sile Doty had met head-on! The confrontation between Frankenstein and Dracula would be nothing in comparison.

Speaking of the clergy, Bourbon whiskey was first distilled by a Presbyterian minister along about 1790. But the frontier didn't have to wait for that particular refinement of the aqua vital art: they had rye whiskey, as celebrated in the famous "Jack of Diamonds" song. This was part of the problem, no doubt. There were times when the price for a gallon of whiskey dropped as low as fifteen and twenty cents. And even in those days, a man could usually raise three nickels from his pocket.

In truth, they didn't know it was loaded. And when whiskey and gunpowder came near each other, the results were often lamentable. In Morgan County, Ohio, some fellows decided upon a wolf hunt. One of them, reporting on the incident, refers to the hunters as being "demoralized by whiskey"—so badly demoralized that one man was shot dead, and another had to hide behind a log to escape the wild barrages that echoed throughout the woods, dribbling leaves and branches upon his head. There was no mention of a wolf being killed. But perhaps this was really incidental, after all.

It was also in Morgan County in the early 1800s that a group of young folks went out skating on the Muskingum River one cold winter day. Someone got the idea that it would be fun to bring a young "crippled" girl out on the ice in a rocking chair and push her along, so that she could share in the fun. But they hit an air pocket, and the girl and rocking chair both disappeared under the ice, not to be seen again for three days, when a young man crossing the bridge looked down and saw the girl's corpse under the ice. Of course, if she had lived to a ripe old age, this girl herself would be dead by now; but as it is, all the progeny she might have had are ghosts. And the thought of her corpse is a terrible and haunting image to remain from such an innocent, heedless, and happy excursion. And a fitting one (in this use of the past) to represent all those other tragic ends to thoughtless moments.

But the figures in the photographs cannot really be ignored or forgotten. Because those cold and formal stances were real, too. They meant something to people, or they wouldn't have been assumed so unanimously. Therefore, they mean something. In fact, they establish a counter truth to that other counter truth I have been emphasizing: the drunken hunters in pursuit of a wolf and the exploding steamboat. America's greatest popular poet of the nineteenth century expressed it very well, when he wrote:

Life is real, life is earnest,
And the grave is not its goal;
Dust thou art to dust returnest
Was not spoken of the Soul.

The poet protests too much, and well he might, for all those schoolboys—the future drunks and gunfighters and daredevils and Lazy Slokanses—needed Longfellow and the McGuffey Readers and Constant Reminders and, yes, those schoolmarms from Connecticut.

Oh, what a dialectic was this! Poker, the world's most popular card game, is an American invention, and during its lusty youth, the sale of a pack of playing cards in Cincinnati was worth a fifty-dollar fine. There is much evidence, however, that the penalty was chronically risked. Mrs. Trollope, who was properly and eloquently shocked by Cincinnati in the early 1800s, was as alarmed by the violence as she was disgusted by the cruel restrictiveness of life there.

BOOKING IN THE HEARTLAND

All these crazy and contradictory things are true, and their accumulative message unmistakable: those people were as various and alive and foolish as we ourselves.

Such a thought brings to mind the best possible use of the past: namely, to know it beyond the simple and exiguous forms of its popular images. To know it in something of its richness and variety. Those superlative crazies I have been discussing are just about all of them splendidly recognizable. You know them, and so do I.

Which is to say, it doesn't do any good to lie about the past or to ignore it and pretend it will go away. It won't; and its ranks are constantly being replenished by people alarmingly like ourselves. There are a lot of good and bad things to know about it. And almost all of them are interesting and potentially useful. You don't even have to go to a country auction to find this out.

Collecting by Chance

In the opening pages of *The Sea and the Jungle,* H. M. Tomlinson tells how he decided to embark upon the long sea voyage that was to become the inspiration for his book. A sailor friend was urging him to go, but Tomlinson couldn't make up his mind. Finally, his friend had an idea:

> "Look here," said the sailor, pointing toward Ludgate Circus, "see that Putney bus? If it takes up two more passengers before it passes this spot, then you've got to come."
>
> That made the difficulty much clearer. I agreed, the bus struggled off, and a man with a bag ran at it and boarded it. One! Then it had a clear run—it almost reached us—in another two seconds!—I began to breathe more easily; the danger of liberty was almost gone. Then the sailor jumped for the bus before it was quite level, and as he mounted the steps, turned, and held up two fingers with a grin.
>
> Thus was a voyage of great moment and adventure begun.

Behind that friend's benevolent trickery, there is a strategy that we all understand. We are familiar with such aleatory gestures; they themselves can free us from the "danger of liberty," upon those occasions when we are intimidated by options. There are times when alternatives are so bewilderingly complex or their consequences so nearly condign that choice seems impossible or irrelevant. Why not flip a coin or base our decision upon which way the cat jumps or which telephone wire a sparrow alights upon? The Romans would have understood this well.

Usually, we think of such devices as appropriate only for trivial decisions: if the waitress comes to the table before the second hand reaches twelve, I'll order the broiled chicken in mushroom sauce; if not, I'll have the Chef's salad. I honestly don't care too much one way or the other, so why not let the waitress decide for me. Rather, not the waitress herself, but her behavior within a whimsical scenario designed for an occasion she knows nothing about.

However, there is the possibility, at least, that aleatory commitments are appropriate for great decisions, as well. Given the machinery that produces a presidential election, a voter is faced with a binary choice, expressible as yes or no, on or off. Although we understand that history may prove a particular choice to be disastrous, history is never present at the critical moment to give testimony. And, of course, the unchosen alternative can never be tested. A flip of the coin is not the worst conceivable strategy for anyone who believes in constitutional democracy, for the machinery is working no matter which candidate is elected; and it is the machinery, after all, that matters.[1]

Aleatory "choice," in which deliberate choice is avoided, seems to be essentially superstitious; and yet, there is another way of looking at it as a response based upon one's understanding of the bewildering complexity of certain human options. It is, or can be, a sign of our unwillingness to choose when the implications of choice are so uncertain that the psychological investment in the act is too great a cost. It is conventional, easy, and usually valid to point out that we should study our alternatives as closely as we can and base our decisions rationally upon the results. But it is also easy to argue that in certain circumstances, faced with certain sorts of alternatives, we should cast our dice and accept the consequences. Caesar did, when he crossed the Rubicon; and, relieved of the anxiety of choice—the "danger of liberty" that Tomlinson refers to—said, *Alea jacta est*—the die is cast. (The first word he uttered is, of course, the root of "aleatory.") Caesar knew about human limitations, and—in this instance, at least—acted accordingly.

The psychological rewards of aleatory choice are considerable. Independent of any rationally defensible premise for belief, there are symbolic reasons for employing it. However entered upon, and whatever the consequences, the quasi fatalism inherent in such behavior is balm to us as we blunder wild-eyed and panting through the daily jungle of decisions. Balm, and something like

1. This argument is not without danger, of course, for *deliberate* choice itself may be said to be part of the "machinery."

sanity. For a moment, we have paused to contemplate our frailty and impoverishment of self-knowledge; we have faced up to and pondered upon how little we know of consequences; and the logical conclusion of this brief change in perspective is a sort of communion with all of the mystery beyond one's self out of that abiding and relentless mystery within.

This, it seems to me, is the essential virtue of aleatory strategies. It acknowledges by means of a single symbolic act the underlying connectedness of the only sorts of truths we know, the inner and outer—the one in which we hide and are always forced to return to in privacy and sleep, and the other which we sense looming over everything we know of the world, demanding constant obedience in its prescribed forms, while the inner stands back in its profound darkness and sucks its thumb. Therefore, in this one gesture, the two become one: our choices are not tests of reality which we are condemned to pass or fail, but rather a participation in one great process of eventuation, where inner motivation and need collaborate with things-as-they-are in the working out of consequences that neither, alone, could fathom or predict. At such moments, we are at home in the world, a condition so uncommon and gratifying, and so integral to what we suppose a valid relation to reality should produce, that it is almost as if the result might justify any premise, no matter how superstitious or irrational.

Nowhere is the mystery of chance more evident than in booking. When I buy an old book, two histories converge, two pasts come together—each translating itself into the form of the other and translated in turn. How does a book "translate" me? It does so by revealing itself only in those places where I have the capacity to see, simultaneously requiring that my responses are adapted to the forms of the text. As in all translations. So that an old tome printed in Latvian or Turkish will not translate me at all, precisely as I am not able to translate it.

The mystery here is not a very great one, and it is not in the least uncommon, but it is worthy of our attention. The convergence of two histories is not peculiar to books—it is true of every convergence. When two people come together, they are two pasts meeting; and the quality of their association—how they "communicate"— will be dependent upon, and indeed a function of, those two constantly burgeoning pasts.

The basis for communication is an area of shared understanding, an overlap in the individual histories of two or more participants. The overlap of a Latvian text of any sort and myself is zero; I simply don't know the language. A seventeenth-century edition of the poems of Edmund Waller and I will overlap much more significantly. Although here, too, there is a translation problem, for the language has changed in myriad ways since that text was inserted into history . . . it's even changed in certain ways since my own insertion into history, not to mention my own changing relationship to the language—which is to say, the way in which, and the degree to which, I may be said to understand it.

Searching among miscellaneous accumulations of books is a near-perfect model of aleatory adventure. When I come upon some obscure book that proves useful and interesting, I am likely to feel the full mystery of the occasion, and, like the old Welshman Glendower, find myself in a world teeming with occult signs. *It was somehow meant to be that this book and I should come together!* Though it may seem deep and mysterious, the awe is not so much philosophical as it is sentimental and superstitious. And there is something poetic about it; although for me the impulse doesn't inspire the writing of real poems laid out like ladders upon the page, but strives to work itself into speculative and fervid prose, such as this you are now reading.

Traveling to estate and yard sales is such a chancy enterprise that aleatory commitments seem only natural. Supposing I am approaching a battery of traffic lights, headed generally for either of two yards sales, both advertising books. One is somewhere ahead and to the right; the other is to the left. As I approach the lights, all lanes are free of traffic. Then, the left-turn light switches to green, while the others remain red. Although I had vaguely thought of going to the sale to the right, because it seemed nearer according to the city map I'd consulted, I do not ignore the cue ahead—I turn left. The traffic signal is a signal in more than one way; it signifies more than the simple fact that at that instant I am legally (and presumably actually) safe in turning left . . . it signifies that circumstances "beyond my control"—things out there in the real world (in contrast to the unreal world inside my head)—might be thought of as participating in the tilting of a genuine, though trivial, dilemma.

Such foolishness, one would suppose, has little to defend it. And the simple truth is, I wouldn't want to plot many of the important decisions I'm faced with upon the random whimsy of the switching system of a traffic control network, which could not take cognizance of my needs even if it wanted to. Nevertheless, for a moment, the machinery of the world and I are in perfect alignment, perfect harmony. When it comes right down to it, I believe in signs, after all; and possibly you do too.

For one thing, almost any inquiry concerning truth leads to some sort of dead end, the deadliest sort of all, without traffic lights or turn-offs. And not the least attraction to superstitions of this sort is the fact that they are interesting. Fun. They are, after all, a sort of game; and we believe in games within their temporal and spatial boundaries—we pretend that they are real and, for the moment, of abiding importance. Such pretense is, of course, essential for success in playing any game, including many that in one perspective or other can be classed among the most serious things we have to do.

But underneath the superstitious minithrill provided by that traffic light's dumb participation in my itinerary is the simple, incontrovertible fact that, insofar as our lives possess linear continuity, all subsequent events in my life will eventually be seen to have been threaded through that particular event as it was determined by the left-turn traffic light. The books I will come upon by means of the left-turn strategy will likely not be the same as those of its alternative, even if I visit both places—assuming that business is good and some books will be purchased at Yard Sale B while I am visiting or traveling to Yard Sale A.

But of course, the implications can be much greater. What if, when I visit Yard Sale A, I encounter a lumber salesman from Seattle who offers to sell me a horse named Alcatraz? He is only a customer like myself; therefore he wouldn't have been there if I hadn't chosen this option first. Or what if there is a storm and a great tulip polar tree is blown down in front of Yard Sale B, where I would have likely parked my car? Or what if I, in arriving at this particular yard sale at this particular time, come upon a book that "changes my life," as they say, and in some important if inscrutable way, helps teach me how to live? *It was as if it were a sign,* we say out of our natural benighted ignorance, and out of our need to feel that things make sense beyond our need itself.

I suspect that a belief in signs is part of everyone's mental baggage. A good indication of this is the availability of the idea as a premise for joking. During a thunderstorm, a man struggles to open a wine bottle; it is particularly stubborn, and he finally growls, "God damn this cork!" At that very instant, there is a sharp crack of thunder, and he looks up and says, "Hey, I'm only kidding!" and everyone laughs. They all know exactly what the utterance means, independently of how consciously or explicitly anyone in the scenario itself might mean it. The meaning is there, and it is inside all of us, even though it leads a secret and latent existence.

I think I may be affected by a belief in magic more than most people . . . or at least something like this sort of magic seems to be nearer the surface of my awareness than I would suppose it is with others. This fact doesn't trouble me greatly, even though I like to think of myself as a basically rational person. Rationally, *per se,* isn't necessarily relevant, for if there are in truth felt forces that interact with what we conventionally suppose to be purely "mental" processes, then it would be something other than rational not to take such forces into account. But this begins to sound too grim, too epistemologically critical—where the issue is somehow "for keeps," and there's no fun at all.

Several years ago on a cold and blizzardy January morning I set out for a town some fifty miles distant, to look at an accumulation of books that sounded very good indeed. I had made the appointment by phone when a woman responded to a newspaper ad I had run. The appointment was firm, and the woman and her husband were planning to meet me at the designated house (not their residence) at 10:30.

Driving out of town I couldn't help noticing how dark and threatening the sky looked. It was perfect blizzard weather—the sort of day you shouldn't plan to travel anywhere, for any reason. The car radio proclaimed this evident truth, and I began to believe that there might be something to it. But the thought of those books (easily aggrandized by a fervid imagination!) made me reluctant to turn back. But after another mile of driving, the imprudence of the venture was obvious, even to me.

I returned to my office so that I could phone the woman and tell her not to go to that house where her books were kept (she had only five or six miles to travel, in contrast to my fifty). I dialed the phone, but it rang busy. I waited a moment and dialed again: still busy. After dialing unsuccessfully four or five times, it came to me: I was *meant* to go, after all. Weather be damned; there were more powerful forces at work.

So I went out to my car, glared at the sky, and started once again toward what seemed my destination in at least two senses. Snow falling, I finally got out on the double highway and felt that the road surface was good—it was covered with packed snow, but seemed relatively free from ice. There appeared to be no trouble with traction, so I put the cruise control on fifty-five and prepared to ride out the trip as far as the turn-off, which I would worry about when the time came.

Then something utterly astonishing happened: without turning the steering wheel a fraction of an inch, without accelerating or decelerating, without hitting a bump or any other sort of deviation in the road's smooth (if icy) surface, the car started to swing in a great leisurely circle. I remember clearly what my sensation was at that first moment when the car had turned, say, forty degrees in its career. My sensation was twofold: it was a philosophical, "Well, this is it!" and, at the same time, it was: "Wheeeeeee!"

By the time the car had turned a full 360 degrees, I was completely off the road, but, of course, faced in my original, intended direction. A pickup had stopped in the highway with its yellow emergency lights flashing. I waved to thank him and negotiated my way back upon the highway, where I continued to the woman's house . . . where I enjoyed a pleasant conversation, then eventually left with a 1711 edition of Swift's *The Tale of a Tub*. Front hinge broken, but otherwise in very good condition. Obviously, even the most sturdy skeptic will now understand (if he knows Swift) how, in truth, this was meant to be. All the signs were for it, weather excepted.

The implications pursuant upon any decision, no matter how arrived at, are marvelous to contemplate. To say that our individual lives, or histories, are evolving systems is to state the obvious. And yet, the implications of the idea, like those of the decisive event, are dismaying in their intricate connectedness. An interesting model is provided by a most-interesting and worthy book, which is only proper. I speak of a book whose title page bears the grand and resounding label:

RUMMY

THAT NOBLE GAME
EXPOUNDED IN PROSE,
POETRY, DIAGRAM AND
ENGRAVING BY
A.E. COPPARD
and
ROBERT GIBBINGS

and continues, "with an account of / certain / Diversions / into / the / Mountain / Fastnesses / of Cork / and Kerry."

This exuberant title page adorns the Golden Cockerel Press edition, limited to 250 copies and signed by both Coppard and Gibbings. It is a very handsome little book with splendid paper, Gibbings's antic illustrations in his best manner, and the text by Coppard worthy of this little-known master of the modern short story. (It should also be mentioned that the letters of "Rummy" are a bright blood red against the rich cream white of the paper and the dense black of the other letters.)

But in addition to the book's physical handsomeness, and more germane to our present theme, is a remarkable dialogue on page 40 (Coppard speaking):

> "Has it ever struck you, Bob, that the sequence in which a pack of cards is packed by the makers is what determines, for good and for all, every subsequent distribution of those cards?"
>
> "Just tell me that once again," he said.
>
> I went over it once more. "It's just luck," he exclaimed.
>
> "So it is," said I. "But all the same, the little boy (or it maybe the little girl) who first packs the new pack of cards in its haphazard order, he it is who may be the innocent cause of your ruin!"
>
> "But aren't they always packed in proper sequence?" he asked.
>
> "I'm surprised at you, Bob! They very seldom are—I don't know why—haven't you ever noticed that?"
>
> "It doesn't make any difference," he answered.
>
> "O, but think of it! The order the cards happen to be in when first bought must influence every deal—you can't get away from it!"

The validity of this intriguing notion seems to me unquestionable, and the implications mind boggling. And yet, we keep on stacking one experience upon another all our days, seldom pausing to contemplate the miraculous complexity of all those evolving universes of discourse opened up casually and relentlessly with each trivial action modifying the previous one and simultaneously establishing the conditions for those that follow.

It would be felicitous to report that I bought *Rummy* on a hot day in Valdosta, Georgia, after turning off the interstate when two semis going up an incline blocked both lanes so that I couldn't pass. But the truth is, I bought it from a fellow collector who had no particular interest in Coppard and was happy to let me have it for a modest price.

But, as the old schoolmen might have argued, this was only the immediate cause for the transaction. Behind that lies the mediate cause, dim in some past occasion when I was young and convinced that I was too poor to collect rare books. Still, I frequented old bookstores, and found a copy of Coppard's *Collected Stories* published sometime in the late 1940s. This was a Book-of-the-Month-Club selection, and it is a title that is still common on the shelves of used books. I remember the deep pleasure I felt when I first read his stories.

I no longer have that particular copy, although I collect Coppard's first editions in a modest way. He is not a hard writer to collect, because the supply is plentiful. He is not popular today, and is not given much critical attention. All of this is too bad, in one sense— but just right in another. The many signed and limited editions of his stories are beautifully printed and the paper is often magnificent. So much artistry in the physical book, and so much artistry within!

But I've drifted from that first occasion when I discovered Coppard by means of a very inexpensive purchase of a very common book. What prompted me to attend to this book instead of all the others surrounding it? Why did the publisher's blurbs influence me in this instance when they can be so easily discounted in others?

It really is something of a mystery, piled upon all those antecedent mysteries. But I have my own theory of what happened: somewhere deep down in the growling machinery of fate, a coin was flipped, and the two of us arranged matters so that I would pick up this particular book and begin to read, as if my life depended upon it.

New Opportunities in Old Books

There is a small class of writers whose effect upon me when I first read their work was to gorge myself upon their books—read a handful right away so that my immediate craving for what they'd done was assuaged. I don't assume for a moment that this experience is unique; in fact, I assume otherwise, for I can't conceive of a serious reader who hasn't come upon an author for the first time and found his or her work so absorbing, so promissory of an entire world of sensibility to be explored with all the adventures of discovery . . . who hasn't launched passionately, excitedly, into that work to find out all that there was to be known through such intense application.

This sort of thing has happened to me with a fairly wide variety of authors. A. E. Coppard and Sigmund Freud, to name an odd couple, were among the first. Even before that, while I was in college, there were Conrad Aiken and Aldous Huxley. Later, there were Thomas Hardy, Dostoevski, John O'Hara (his short stories), Anthony Burgess, Patrick White, Robertson Davies . . . and, no doubt, others I can't think of at the moment. (If this partial list seems to be symptomatic of a badly fragmented personality, no matter. These are all writers who have fired my imagination at one time or other, and I honor them for the fact.)

The personal "discovery" of a writer does not necessarily eventuate in collecting his or her work: I collect A. E. Coppard, but not Freud. But one writer who has inspired this sort of overdosing, and whose first editions I do collect, is the mystery writer, John D. MacDonald, whose faults (sexist stereotypes he strives only halfheartedly to conceal, clichés of modern *Angst*, easy philosophizing that sometimes works, sometimes doesn't) are on the surface, but whose virtues are as genuine as . . . well, *the real thing*. His novels are impressively inventive within the mapped-out area where his preoccupations and his chosen *genre* intersect; they are filled with the lovingly detailed paraphernalia of our bureaucracies—he writes more convincingly and enthusiastically about insurance frauds, investment strategies, tax finessing, gambling odds, and con games than any other writer whose work I know.

Also, in the friendship of Travis McGee (the "salvage consultant" detective whose adventures are celebrated in a long series of novels) and a squat, hairy economist named Meyer, there is celebrated a human attachment that is realized with rare and convincing pleasure—a thoroughly heterosexual companionship between males whose trust and liking for each other is convincingly demonstrated in all sorts of ways, revealing the comfort and satisfaction of such a "relationship" that is based upon simple liking and trust, but relieved of the static and excitement of sexual attraction.

MacDonald is far from being my own private discovery, although I am not aware of any significant critical attention given to his work; and the dust jacket blurbs are so ho-hum that they might apply to a hundred lesser writers who do more or less "the same sort of thing." Still, his mysteries are, so far as I can tell, best-sellers in every sense of the term. Fawcett generally publishes them first; then a hardcover edition—at least in recent years—tends to follow. Lippincott has been his hardcover publisher up until 1985, when *The Lonely Silver Rain* was brought out by Knopf.

In spite of huge paperback printings and general popularity, I think that the first editions of MacDonald are well worth collecting; I collect them in both paperback and cloth, and reread them occasionally . . . doing so with pleasure, which is one of the tests of literary merit, for rereadability in a book is rare, indeed—especially with regard to mysteries, which (we are often told) depend so much upon plot. But of course, my contention here is that much more than plot is happening in MacDonald's books—excellent as his plots generally are—and this additional factor is what gives him special status as a writer . . . and makes him, if we are once again driven to use the offensive word, *collectible*.

A small percentage of today's popular writers will last on for a while—how long depends, of course; and nobody knows exactly what it depends *on*. There is another class of generally unrecognized writers who will be plucked out of general anonymity and recognized as having had a special and worthwhile perspective into the human condition in this lively and frolicsome era. Such rediscovery may not take place until a century after they are dead (we can hardly wait); but there is always the possibility that it will happen, even after years of decline in the authority of the printed word and the integrity of the text.

But it is pusillanimous for a book lover to spend much time entertaining fantasies concerning the evanescence of print. The world is full of books, and among them are inconceivable treasures awaiting all of us if we know where, and how, to look. Such treasures are of two sorts: named and unnamed . . . those which have been identified as treasures, institutionalized as "literature" (or history or philosophy or science), and are therefore desirable in the form they were known by at the moment of their insertion into time—which is to say their first, or otherwise noteworthy, editions.

Within the vast and changing "language game" that all of us are forced to play (always, even to ourselves in private dialogue) are manifold subgames. And, to paraphrase Swift in his poem on fleas and jealous poets, "these have further still to bite 'em, and so it goes, *ad infinitum.*" Most of our conventions and proprieties, which is to say, our values, are structured as subgames within the language.

One subgame that I am familiar with is the teaching of English literature in college. I make my living as a professor of English, and I am often reminded of how tentative and arbitrary literary reputations can prove. Twenty years ago, Herman Melville's "Bartleby, the Scrivener" was everyone's great short story; and there was actually a conference of scholars focused upon this single work and the critical thought it had by that time inspired. It is, in truth, a masterful tale; but its worth cannot be traced by the wild upsurge in its popularity as a literary enigma yearning toward explication, and its present relative neglect. It is only in games that such shifts can be observed in precisely this way; but in this game, as in so many that demand judgment and evaluation of us, we hardly know who the players are or what is at stake; and we find ourselves groping to understand the rules even after the game seems to be over.

The intimate relationship between the world of rare books and college-level courses in the humanities is a critical one, in more than one sense. To a great extent, the books we as collectors cherish and covet are those that have been institutionalized as important documents in the history of our kind. Even illustrated and lavishly produced private press books, which might seem exempt from this historically oriented premise, will be valuable to the extent that their artistry is generally acknowledged to be worthwhile. Social arbitrariness, when intensely focused and prolonged, ceases to be what we usually think of as "arbitrary" . . . for one thing, it can translate into hard cash—but then, a currency system is itself a subgame and therefore dependent upon arbitrariness sustained by whole populations and generations of tacit consensus.

The currency of English departments throughout colleges and universities is subject to some of the same forces that affect monetary systems: we speak of one author's reputation as inflated and the work of another as sound; we identify a neglected author as one to whom greater critical attention is due, and easily perceive that the values implicit in older literary works are no longer negotiable. Fashions in literary reputations are at times notoriously short-lived, and collectors with an eye upon investment do well to look around them and try to see which way the world is headed. Just like other investors.

The most volatile area in collecting is, of course, that of modern and contemporary literature. Thirty years ago, people were scrambling for first editions of J. D. Salinger and Dylan Thomas. Today, the market for both of these writers—passionately lionized in the 1950s—has sagged. Will they be "rediscovered," thus vindicating those collectors who invested in their works? Before that happens, some astute and authoritative critic will have to read them again with something of the entranced surprise that their first readers experienced. They will have to be reassessed, and their works somehow *placed*—which is to say, categorized and graded—in the canon of twentieth-century literature.

Part of the pleasure in collecting is to build your own literary curriculum. Rediscovering an old and neglected writer is something of a personal triumph, after all. Such a writer need not be a "new discovery" in the sense that no one has ever heard of his or her work. There is a natural sag in a writer's reputation, no matter how gifted. Who today collects the first editions of Conrad Aiken, Willa Cather, William Dean Howells, Edith Wharton, Sherwood Anderson, or, even, Emerson? It is astonishing, as well as gratifying to the bargain-minded collector, that these writers are generally as neglected in the rare book market (which is not to say *entirely* neglected) as they are in the classrooms.

Among those listed above, there are two women. Why, in view of the recent preoccupation with, and ascendancy of, feminine consciousness, haven't their books risen sharply in value? There are three possible answers, not mutually exclusive: one, the male-dominated establishment has not been as sexist as one would suppose; two, collectors simply haven't come awake to the fact of their literary worth and theoretical collectibility; three, most collectors are still men, and *as* men, they instinctively shy away from female writers.

One of the joys of collecting is the adventure of discovery. You can never know enough about even a single author; in view of this, think of the prodigies of information, insight, wisdom, and simple down-home enchantment that await those who sort through great miscellaneous accumulations of old books if they only take time to pause and read from them now and then!

A little over a year ago, at an AAUW sale, I bought a copy of the bound galleys of *High Sierra*, by W. R. Burnett. It was in such excellent condition that it seemed a shame not to pick it up for a quarter. Bound galleys are a sort of "first edition of the first edition"—for, as their name signifies, they are galley sheets that are bound up before publication, and even before the first trade copies are bound in cloth. These are special copies that are sewn and fixed with paper covers so that they can be sent to the few special review media that run the early reviews—*Publisher's Weekly, Library Journal, The Kirkus Review*—along with special early copies to some of the major newspapers and book clubs.

Having the *first* first edition of *High Sierra* struck me as a special opportunity, providing I could respect the book. I had, of course, heard of Burnett, but associated him (as I suppose most people do) with two movies made from his novels: *Little Caesar*, starring Edward G. Robinson, and *High Sierra*, starring Humphrey Bogart. Wouldn't it be ironic if a virtually forgotten author, remembered—if remembered at all—primarily because of two movies, featuring major stars, made from his fiction . . . wouldn't it be nice if such an author would prove worthy *as* an author—which is to say, on his own, as a story teller of the written word?

Entertaining this fantasy, I began to think that if such a happy discovery *were* being prepared for me, I would really want to keep that paperbound galley in its present fine condition. So I went to the library at Ohio University, where I teach, and borrowed the old and tattered copy of *High Sierra*—one that I couldn't help noticing had not circulated for more than a decade.

At this juncture, the question has to arise: was I so intent upon preparing for a literary treat that the reading of Burnett's book would almost inevitably provide a special pleasure? Would any delight it provided be something in the way of a self-fulfilling prophecy? No one is possessed of the self-knowledge necessary for a categorical denial of a charge like this. And yet, I have approached hundreds of old books in a hopeful spirit; and needless to say, the reading of only a few pages has almost always turned that hopefulness to despair. In case anyone needs convincing, I am ready to swear that it is merciful that most books are forgotten.

But such, as you will anticipate, was not the case with *High Sierra*, which proved to be a powerful, fascinating work. It seemed to me that, in this book alone, Burnett proved himself to be a master of the plain style and (much as I dislike the term) what is called "the proletarian novel." If you do not instinctively care for the plain style and the *milieu* of small-town, middle America, you may not grasp what is especially vivid and true—which is to say, universal— in Burnett's fiction. He is in the tradition of Sherwood Anderson and Hemingway (although he and Hemingway were born in the same year); he is also, in certain obvious ways, akin to Chandler, Hammett, Cain, and all those writers of the tough-guy school of the thirties. The baroque or gothic *tour de force*, featuring relentlessly radical juxtaposition, that is fashionable in so much contemporary fiction is alien to the stark and powerful simplicity of Burnett's novels.

Practically unknown, certainly uncanonized, Burnett was a remarkable writer. Upon first reading *High Sierra* I was inspired to go to other novels he had written; and I was not disappointed. Burnett joined the ranks of Hardy, Freud, MacDonald, et al., as one of those writers whose work I had to read immediately. I was intrigued and eager to know as much of his fiction as I could reach. Therefore, I went back to the university library, then to the county library, finding several more titles and reading them . . . and finally running an ad in *AB Bookman's Weekly*, soliciting quotes for any books by Burnett, W. (for William) R. (for Riley). The response was lively, and I was able to buy first edition copies of *Dark Hazard, Iron Man, Vanity Row,* and *Dark Command*—all of which I promptly read with great enthusiasm and pleasure, and then added to my collection of modern first editions.

It is always difficult to convey a sense of the specific virtues of a writer you admire, and this is especially true of one who writes in the plain style so admired in the thirties and forties. By definition, such a writer cannot be quoted as effectively as, say, Faulkner—one of whose sentences from "The Bear" or *As I Lay Dying* might well carry something of the high rhetoric in the writer's signature. The plain style is by definition not representable by tropes and figures, syntactic configurations, or image patterns. It is hardly possessed of such virtues. Its effects are cumulative, entering the text unobtrusively in the form of scene inventories, denoted actions, and things literally done and said in dialogue. It also relies upon larger narrative configurations: the dramatic eventuations that mark the major turns of the story, along with the relentless revelation of idea and character in the telling of how one thing leads to another.

However, if I had to choose from what I have read of Burnett's work a single passage that seems to me representative of his full strength as a writer, I would go to a scene near the end of his novel *Iron Man.* To understand it fully, one would of course have to read the entire novel. But in lieu of this, one should at least know that the "Iron Man" of the title is a prizefighter in the 1920s (the book was published in 1930), named Coke Mason, who has been middleweight champion of the world. But now, near the end of the book, he is being brutally and systematically demolished by a younger fighter named O'Keefe. He is aware that he has already lost, and also aware that his wife has betrayed him, that she has left him; and yet he loves her as much as ever, which is almost to simple-mindedness. All of this is to some degree present in his mind as he sags, badly beaten and numb from pain, in his corner between the eighth and ninth rounds:

> Coke felt a sudden lassitude; he felt old and worn out. He wished it was all over; then he could go home and lie in the dark. He glanced up at the powerful white light over the ring. Beyond that was a cloudy, summer sky. He could see the flash of matches in the far off bleacher seats. He glanced down into the ringside. Men were staring at him with set faces. Did they know it was all over?

The "flash of matches" as the spectators sitting far away light cigars and cigarettes is, I believe, a detail of majestic power, for it brings almost all that has happened to Coke Mason into a single, transfixing image.

Speaking of his own work, as quoted in *Authors Today and Yester-*

day (New York, 1934), Burnett said, "Working toward a purely objective type of writing, I select simple types; types not unduly influenced by thought. The gang leader in *Little Caesar,* Rico, is an extremely simple man. He wants power; he goes after it in a beeline. Coke Mason in *Iron Man* is equally simple, but more natural than Rico, more human . . . dominated by his love for his wife. Both failed thru [*sic*] their simplicity. They cannot stand half measures and like Ibsen's Brand demand all or nothing."

This is, of course, one version of the tragic hero; and Coke Mason embodies it with impressive conviction. He is believable even today, in spite of Burnett's use of dated slang and the reliance that all writers must have upon readers who can immediately recognize the world he is writing about and from. Most contemporary readers will have to make the proper adjustments, just as they must do with the stories of Fitzgerald and Hemingway; but there is a real world of the imagination there, for those who can see what is visible and hear what is audible, even after all these years.

Occasionally, after attempts to "rediscover" some long forgotten or long-neglected author, the almost inevitable failure is disheartening. People seem content not to be disturbed in revising old judgments of literary worth. There's hardly room for a "new classic" for readers who have forgotten Smollett and are forgetting Thackeray. Twenty years ago, a new edition of Matthew G. Lewis's old gothic novel, *The Monk,* was issued; but I don't think it accomplished much. I don't know of its ever being "taught" in any courses in late eighteenth-century literature (where I suppose it belongs), nor do I actually know of anyone who has read it. Still, it was praised extravagantly, and perhaps accurately. A sorry tale, indeed.

And yet, *The Monk* was reborn for a while; and beyond doubt, this brief flurry of critical attention had some effect. When I came upon a copy of Lewis's *Journal of a West India Proprietor in the Island of Jamaica* (London, 1834), I did the right thing—I bought it and then read it, and valued it sufficiently to have it rebacked, for the old leather spine had rotted away. It was a pleasurable book to read, and I doubt if I would have done so if some of that relatively recent praise for *The Monk* had not been echoing in my head.

This may be the best that can be hoped for; but it is not inconsiderable, in the nature of mortal things. Lewis was a natural writer to be ignored and neglected; he had a gift for such things, as many of us do—some deservedly so, some not quite. And the obvious thing has to be said: that my own testimony is only partial; and if Lewis's

BOOKING IN THE HEARTLAND

Journal did not inspire me to raid his works, hungry to absorb them all, it might have affected someone else quite differently, and no doubt there are handsome Matthew G. Lewis collections on various shelves somewhere in the world. And some of these may have resulted from the by-now almost forgotten "rediscovery."

Lewis's work is said to have had a significant influence upon the early poetry of Sir Walter Scott. Perhaps the time is fast approaching when even quasi-educated readers will have to ask who *Scott* was; but that is something I don't want to contemplate just yet.

The Wear of Time

**R**ecently I bought a bumped, tattered, and torn copy of Samuel Cummings's *The Western Pilot*. This is a wonderful old book published for the use of steamboat, keelboat, and flatboat pilots in navigating the Ohio and Mississippi rivers in the early 1800s. The first edition, printed in Philadelphia in 1822, was titled *The Western Navigator*, and came out in two volumes. In his *US-iana*, Wright Howes states that there were over twenty subsequent printings under various titles, and reports that "in later issues Cumings' [sic] name was replaced by those of the publishers—Conclin or James. Poetic justice to one whose book was based, without credit, on Cramer's " 'Navigator.' " Then Howes assigns an "aa" value to any of these reprints, such being his code for books in the $25 to $100 price range . . . a considerable rarity in 1962 when Howes's second (and last) edition was published.

The Cramer referred to was named Zadok. Ostensibly, the first and second editions of his *The Ohio and Mississippi Navigator* were published in two volumes (as was Cummings's first edition) in 1798. But no copy of either edition is now known to exist, even though Evans cites them, and Zadok Cramer's earliest known edition (Pittsburgh, 1802) is labeled the third. From the appearance of my Cummings edition published in Cincinnati in 1837, it is not hard to believe that all copies of the first two editions could have disappeared.

This book was printed for practical use by riverboatmen on the frontier, and if my relatively recent copy has been nearly thumbed to oblivion, what must have been the fate of those earlier printings, the first of which were used exclusively by flatboatmen, who lived as rough a life as just about any life heard of? It is not surprising that most copies remaining from those two dozen editions, both Cramer's and Cummings's, should be dilapidated, for the great majority were consulted roughly in all sorts of weather, handled and mauled in the urgency of the moment (the Ohio River Falls swiftly approaching, for example), by men whose hands were thick and hard as horn from their handling the poles and sweeps. Being viewed as solely functional, copies were tossed overboard or used to start a fire when a more recent edition, with corrections and fresh information about shifting sandbars and shallowing channels, was available. However, its solidly practical character and its lack of pretentiousness or concern for posterity provide most that is interesting in this fascinating book.

My copy is in beggarly condition. It was bound in boards with a leather spine, but the leather is cracked and mostly gone, and the boards have been worn to a soft and discouraged dullness, with the consistency of a baked sweet potato that has been inscrutably flattened. Most of the print has been rubbed off, so that the words *Western Pilot* seem to be impressed in the substance of time itself.

The title page asserts that this is a "New Edition," not simply a reprint, and that it has in fact been edited, by which we are to infer that there is up-to-date information about the more ephemeral landmarks and features of the rivers' shorelines, such as new villages, or those with extended boundaries, new ferries, newly constructed cabins, newly cleared land, and even isolated trees that have grown vast enough to fix bearings on—anything that could serve as a guide one day, but might be gone or changed beyond recognition the next.

Much like editions themselves. Wright Howes does not distinguish my 1837 edition from the other reprints of the first (1822) edition, but he should have. While it is true that the words "revised" or "new edition" on a title page cannot always be taken literally to mean substantive changes from earlier printings, this 1837 edition of Cummings's classic of riverboat lore is tangibly possessed of fresh information.

We are told as much in the "Advertisement," placed and dated, "Cincinnati, June, 1837," and further informed that: "During the low water of last year, (1836), Captains Charles Ross and Hugh M'Clain undertook to examine the Ohio and Mississippi Rivers, from Pittsburgh to New Orleans, with the view of ascertaining the exact situation of the channels, and pointing out the manner of running them."

That this is not mere applesauce is everywhere evident. In his description of Cincinnati, Cummings writes: "The city is advancing with rapid march in population, wealth, and improvements of every description. Within the last year, (1836), six hundred new buildings were erected, many of which are large, expensive, and elegant. It contains at present 4000 houses, and 37,000 inhabitants." Such enumerative precision does not astonish us, but it gives evidence of careful survey. If you are going to lie in print, it's best to avoid specificity and be judiciously vague.

Current information abounds. Consider the following entry for Three Mile Island Dam, downriver from Cincinnati, given in its entirety:

> The dam commences on the left shore, nearly a mile below the island. It runs quartering down and across within 200 yards of the right shore, a very small distance above Lane's wood yard. The best water (1835–6) was through the gap or breach in the dam about 150 yards from the left shore. When below about 300 yards, opposite a small clearing on the left, turn and go over to the right shore. In all probability Capt. Shrieve will have this breach repaired soon; then you will keep it close on your left until you get in to shore. Here is a round topped tree; a tolerably good mark—when you go to the right of the dam, this tree is on the right shore opposite the foot of the dam and about 150 yards above the upper wood yard.

Such folksy directions are possessed of more charm than comfort. Certainly, there would have been little comfort for steamboat passengers, brooding over the uncertainty of the things of this world, in knowing that such whimsical details were relied upon for guidance. What would happen if Lane went out of business or moved his wood yard before the next edition of *The Western Pilot* appeared? What would the captain take his bearings from if somebody chopped down that "round topped tree"? Would Capt. Shrieve repair his breach in time?

Sternly utilitarian in purpose, *The Western Pilot* is wildly poetic, even when it is trying to be most matter of fact. One is delighted by the mere listing of the names encountered on the descent of the great rivers from Pittsburgh to New Orleans. Their quaintness and primitive vigor are in many instances still with us, for some names have lasted on, even into our world. The mixture is perfect, for it includes exotic Indian words with simple Anglo-Saxon tags that evoke a crude and bloody history.

Just below Pittsburgh is Dead Man's Island (a story in that, you would think), and then such places as Big Bone Lick Creek and Conoconneque Creek. This last is surely a variation upon *kinnikinnick,* a generic Algonquin term referring to various bark mixtures for smoking (the word originally means "mixture"). This term was especially familiar in the Ohio Valley, and there is still a "Knick Kneck Creek" in Ross County, Ohio.

Truly, the march of names is grand. You can read them on the river maps that chart their way through Cummings's old book: Hockhocking River, the Great Kenhawa River, Bogg's Island, Big Grave Creek, Sisterville, Virginia (now West Virginia) with a "Petticoat Ripple" nearby. Then there is Scuffletown Bar, not to mention Sprinklesburgh, Shawneetown, and Paducah.

Once out on the Mississippi, you meet Bloody Island ("Channel to the right," is its sole entry), Hanging Dog Island, Iron Banks, and near New Orleans, the Yazoo Bayou. Not to mention 12 Pole Island and Riddle's Point (with "an ugly bar on the right below the point"). Riverboatmen were known for their hard drinking—which often led to death by knife, gunshot, drowning, or nightmare—but even if they were sober, all of those names would have been enough to inspire them to giddiness and wonder.

But there is one name that perplexes me entirely. Somewhere downriver from Cooper's Ferry, New London, Bethlehem, and West Port is a place called Hark Linnen. What is it? I don't know. To the right of each entry throughout the book are two vertical columns with channel depth in fathoms in the first and miles downriver from Pittsburgh in the second. The columns beside Hark Linnen, whatever it is, have been left blank. No channel? I doubt it. No distance from Pittsburgh? I doubt that too, since West Port, immediately preceding, is 590½ (miles), with a channel depth of six fathoms.

Exactly what is "Hark Linnen"? Whatever it is, it is on the right side of the river as you descend, and the river there is described as follows:

> Mouth of Bull creek on the right. At the mouth of Bull Creek is Hark Linnen, wear in within one third of the right hand shore and keep down about a mile and a half, then wear in close to the right and keep within 50 yards of the shore. About a mile and a half below Hark Linnen is grass flats, channel at either side, but the best channel to the right at low water. Now keep to the middle of the river until you come

to the head of Twelve Mile Island, then wear in within one third of the shore, between the island and the shore, until past the island.

Well, perhaps it is a town. Let's say it is, even though it isn't listed on any contemporary map of Kentucky that I know about. In addition, there is the mystery of its being mentioned without further reference. It isn't even on Map # 13, facing the page. There is one other singular feature in this entry: the odd use of the metaphor "wear in" for "approach and run parallel to."

But all of the entries are interesting: some stylistically so, some interesting because of their insights into an old and forgotten time (insights that only old books can give), and others interesting because of their colorful detail.

But even the most terse and functional directions come to us out of a context of hard usefulness. My copy, like most encountered, has been held in hands chilled by frozen wind spray from the river, or by hands that have just laid down the playing cards in the lantern light, in order to consult where Ferguson's Bar or Bullskin Creek has managed to hide out there in the darkness.

It's no wonder that *The Western Pilot* is a classic of riverboat Americana.

There is a reason for my emphasis upon the desperately poor condition of my copy of Cummings's old tome. Collectors of antiquarian books are virtually unanimous in their insistence upon good condition. No matter how old, a book should be fresh, clean, and whole. As near fine as possible.

There is a contrary principle, however, that works against the premium attached to excellent condition. That is that of authenticity. "Original boards" is an obligatory feature for many collectors; and no one can doubt the unique pleasure one feels in holding an early eighteenth-century book in fine condition—bound with inlaid calf, hinges firm and tight, and heavy rag paper with the type as palpably impressed as braille in the texture of the page.

Being of this world (at least those who *are*), collectors must upon occasion face up to the possibility of sensible compromise. If you collect antiquarian books, and you are interested in some of the great rarities, you will soon reach the point where you will compromise or desist. What does compromise mean in this context? Well, settle for a less-than-perfect copy, for instance. One in "fair" (i.e., poor) or "poor" (wretched) condition.

This may be judicious, or it may not. I recently turned down a first edition of *Moby Dick*, priced at only $700, because its binding was battered and torn. Of course, I might have had it rebound handsomely for $50, but what, exactly, would I have had afterwards? Some books (many Americana titles, for example) might be rebound with little or no loss in value; and I have a first English edition of Poe's *Poetical Works* (London, 1853) rebound by Sangorski and Sutcliff. But somehow, this seems all right, even proper, whereas Melville's great classic should not be altered in this way, in my opinion; although I'm not sure why such a distinction seems valid.

Often a collector will compromise by retaining the original binding, no matter how loathsomely worn, while supplying a specially made, often handsomely designed, case for the book. Probably whoever bought that copy of *Moby Dick* would be advised to do something like this. But even then, the mixture seems a bit odd, makeshift, and oblique to the ideals of collecting.

Are there any books, under any circumstance, that should be kept—perhaps even proudly or defiantly—in battered condition? I think there is a very small class of such books, and to argue for this exception is not at all to ignore or impugn the principle of "good to fine condition." I am, of course, talking about books whose very purpose for being was practical; I am talking about useful books, that might legitimately show signs of having been used; I am talking about books that are "distressed," in the manner of antique furniture, where evidence of age and long, hard service are judged not merely allowable, but desirable. I am talking about such books as Cummings's *The Western Pilot*.

In this context, and perhaps in this context alone, the analogy between rare books and antique furniture is valid. A double standard seems to exist, whereby we view with distrust and even contempt a first edition of Dickens that has been "read to death," whereas a similarly damaged or worn first edition copy of Josiah Gregg's *Commerce of the Prairie* may be valued somewhat according to, or even in proportion to, those signs of hard use that are not acceptable in a novel.

Why should this be so? I'm not sure; however, there might be something in the idea that a work of art is in an odd sort of way "timeless," even while it gives voice and vividness to the world it expresses; whereas the functional book speaks sturdily and directly to the historical occasion that brought it forth.[1] The account books of a canal boat, for example, lose all practical value the instant that boat ceases to run; and this loss is italicized when the canals themselves cease to exist. Being in and of a particular time, some books take upon themselves the signature of age; while other books, being works of art (as we say), are somehow viewed as exempt from the cost of centuries and seasons.

Is this sentimental nonsense? Maybe. But then, such an ugly label can be attached to the very idea of collecting old and rare books, especially the passion for first editions. And no healthy-minded collector is about to pay serious attention to such an argument, for if this sort of thinking can carry us this far, practically all that we covet for mysterious reasons will be cheapened, right before our eyes, including that least serviceable treasure of all, gold.

One of the requirements for collecting rare books successfully is an attentive eye. As in the study of literature, the gift and discipline of passionate attention is essential. Sometimes what is discovered will afterwards appear obvious; but this is not unusual. Certainly, the badly worn condition of my copy of Cummings's *The Western Pilot* should not be perplexing. This is not a book that has suffered through neglect: it has not been thrown in a box in some shed, where mice and silverfish have fed upon its traces of animal fat in the glue. It is a book that has been leafed, fumbled, flipped through, and cursed at . . . all in the urgency of necessity, if not action.

One sign of this is the curious fact that my copy of *The Western Pilot* is most horribly mutilated on the leaves beginning with Map # 14 (p. 51) through Map # 15 (p. 54). These pages are badly torn, with the upper right section of the recto leaves waterstained. It is true, as it is in the nature of things, that these water stains are not limited to the above-mentioned leaves, but the tears are.

That this should be the case is not surprising, for this section of Cummings's book is devoted to what used to be called "The Falls of the Ohio." The map shows the river swollen as it descends to Louisville. Two channels are marked by arrows pointing downstream, one on each side of Corn Island. Small x's are everywhere, indicating rocks; they thicken like flies on the forearm of a corpse on the

1. Literature, according to George Steiner, "is language in some degree outside ordinary time." *Extraterritorial* (New York, 1971), p. 128.

approach to Goose Islands, little symbols of mathematical uncertainty.

The swift current, the rapids, the shallows and bars populate the riverman's nightmare. And yet, the Louisville and Portland Canal had been built by this time: its ruler-straight line cuts off the river's great dangerous swing, which had already wrecked so many flatboats, keelboats, barges, and steamboats in those early days.

What can we infer by this? Is it likely that this copy of *The Western Pilot* was used by flatboatmen who could pole their way past all those perils more easily than a deep-drawing steamboat could? This is plausible enough. Certainly, a boat that took the canal would not have given cause to consult those specific pages, leaving so much evidence of hard usage.

Or perhaps some of this, some of that. The river changes, and always has: that's why the book required periodic reprints, to reflect these changes of landmark and bottom. But there was an awful lot of traffic on the rivers in those days, and no doubt some out-of-date copies were in use long after their relevance. You can almost hear one of the captains saying, "What it says about the left channel by Otter Creek isn't good any more. That tobacco landing you're supposed to steer by hasn't been there for twenty years."

We see traces of time everywhere, and no particular cunning is required to understand such signs. A pencil gets shorter and carries its fate with it, right up to the nub that will be thrown away. Hair turns gray and the flesh sags; all things wear out in their time, imprinted with the beat of circadian clocks that measure just about all the changes we can understand.

Implements from the past come to us out of their depth, and we say that it's only right that they should show evidence of their journey. The journey of Cummings's old classic originated in a time when sentiment and romantic wonder (such as are celebrated in this piece) were respected for the truth they conveyed along with their ability to exalt, to heighten, the human adventure.

Thus it is appropriate to quote from Cummings's description of the Ohio river just above The Falls, the very section—of book and river—we have been contemplating. In spite of that sternly utilitarian character that I have so often mentioned, this passage will reveal that no context was too alien for a brief romantic interlude with language and a mighty vista:

The falls may be seen from the town, and present a romantic appearance. The river is divided by a fine island, which adds to the beauty of the scene. In high stages of water, the falls almost entirely disappear; but when the water is low, the whole width of the river, which is here nearly a mile wide, has the appearance of a great many broken rivers of foam, making their way over the falls.

If Cummings and his readers could pause to indulge sensibility and despise exigency, so surely can we, after all this time. And while it is evident that our view is only dimly reflective of what Cummings saw and tried to describe, there is nevertheless another dimension afforded us, and we would be foolish to ignore it. I speak of the signature of time itself upon this old navigational guide.

The time it bears witness to has traveled all this way, and the generations of men who have handled it and consulted it in sunlight and by lantern, to work their way through winter storms, spring rains, and the peaceful and fragrant air of summer and autumn . . . they have left their imprint upon these pages as well, and such mute testimony is vivid and precise even if we can't read it as we do that other text.

Cincinnatus Redivivus, or
George Washington Redone

The onus of practicality lies heavy upon us, and it is not surprising that quixotic endeavors are often possessed of a certain odd majesty. I think of grandiose undertakings, defiant in their uselessness: a plant to convert fresh water into salt; a lighted parking lot in Nevada, unconnected with any road; the writing of a subtle and deep novella, devoid of the thrills afforded by the pop lit equivalent of a motorcycle chase.

The list could be extended indefinitely. How about carving a perfect cow out of butter, translating the works of Germaine Greer into classical Greek, or perhaps writing (not translating) the life of Washington in Ciceronian Latin. Launch upon any list of outrageously improbable enterprise, and you will soon run aground upon some shoal of fact.

And the relevant fact in this enterprise is that there was once a man named Francis Glass who did in truth write a biography of George Washington in Latin. Glass was an impoverished schoolmaster "from the backwoods of Ohio," and his *Washingtonii Vita* was not only written; it was published in Harper's in 1835, eleven years after Glass had died.

Probably no idiosyncrasy stands entirely alone, which is to say that, literally speaking, there are no true idiosyncrasies at all, merely samples taken from a continuum that extends from some conventional center of gravity to airy centrifugal flickers beyond any established circumference of reasonable expectation. What was that? Well, let's say there is, in the context of contemporary publishing, the predicted best-seller of some quasi-literate celebrity's memoirs to a novel on the dream life of Herbert Hoover . . . and in terms of predictability, all sorts of titles in between, decreasing in likelihood as they drift from the first class and approach the second.

While writing a book in Latin seems idiosyncratic to us, it makes a special claim upon our imaginations (our linearity begins to curve, here), so that if a translation of *Winnie the Pooh* or *Ferdinand the Bull* is published, the mere extravagance of the enterprise proves beguiling. You like to have a copy on your coffee table as a curiosity on the order of a Shoshone bear claw necklace or one of Elvis Presley's neckties. You don't even have to read Latin. In fact, it may be better if you don't.

Winnie Ille Pooh and *Ferdinandus Taurus* have been published, and have gained for themselves a brief popularity as items of minicult. They are jokes, partaking of the monumental irrelevance of the study of Latin itself, in conjunction with the greatly relevant, if somewhat looked-down-on, institution of juvenile entertainment. The juxtaposition is meant to create a sense of bathos and whimsy; the linguistic means (representative of all that is difficult and recondite) devoted to an end we view as innocent and simple. Like killing a mosquito with a garden spade or delivering a five-gallon can of nosedrops to someone with a head cold.

Latin translations of standard works are not new. In a grumpy review of *Winnie Ille Pooh,*[1] Gilbert Highet refers to Latin translations of *Pinnochio (Pinoculus), Alice in Wonderland,* and *The Hunting of the Snark.* But he expresses severe disapproval of *Ille Pooh,* critical of its Latinity. His essay, signed "Gilbertus Criticus," ends resoundingly with the statement: "When a thing is intended to be useless, it ought at least to be elegant."

Modern Latin translations of well-known books or stories must necessarily be regarded as "useless," of course, for the vehicle is itself believed to be useless. Very much as horseback riding is useless in a time when even a bicycle provides better transportation. But such an enterprise was not always so regarded; Latin translations of currently popular works had at one time the excuse of helping the uninterested young learn Latin. If they couldn't "get into" Caesar or Pliny, well they surely could learn to find *Robinson Crusoeus* interesting. Not only interesting, but with a readily available pony.

There have been at least four Latin translations of DeFoe's great adventure classic. One, by Joachim Heinrich Campe, is evidently a

---

1. *Horizon,* July, 1961.

translation from the German, *Robinson der Jungere*. Another, done by Francis William Newman and published in 1884, is given the sturdy, honest title: *Rebilius Cruso: Robinson Crusoe in Latin: A Book to Lighten Tedium to a Learner*. (I have no idea what *rebilius* might signify, but the rest is clear; and as a teacher I am well aware of how important it is to lighten tedium to any learner in sight.) Still another translation, anonymous, is titled *Robinson Crusoeus, Sermone Anglico Scriptit Daniel Defoe*—also honest, in its way, for it states that DeFoe (first) wrote the text in English.

Perhaps it doesn't seem so odd that DeFoe's classic was translated into Latin; there are, after all, editions in virtually all languages, including Latvian and Persian. Still, there are Latvians and Persians (Iranians) still around to read the book; but there are no Romans, at least none of those whose native language is Latin. Clearly, these translations were done for pedagogical reasons, or for pecuniary reasons ostensibly directed towards pedagogical goals. They were done in a time when it was believed that learning Latin was an intellectual exercise that improved the mind, rendering it supple, informed, and resourceful. Later, this idea was repudiated; but since that time, even the repudiation has become irrelevant, and if one were to think hard upon the matter, the original notion might prove to have some merit. Learning Latin probably does improve one's intellect, in the sense of "developing" it, although not as directly and simply as was once believed.

We seem to have strayed a good distance from Francis Glass and his biography of George Washington. It must be emphasized that this is not a translation—certainly not a translation of Parson Weems's classic, which had been often reprinted by the time of Glass's death, so that in 1835 the cherry tree story was already part of our national myth. (Glass does not mention the cherry tree, of course, for it never existed, except in Weems's feverish notions.)

Curious as it is, Glass's book is nevertheless a product of a familiar enterprise: old methods for teaching Latin gave almost as much emphasis to translating English into Latin as translating Latin into English. This fact bears repeating. It was thought that such transactional exercises gave students a feel for Latin that couldn't be gotten in other ways. Therefore, there is a whole tradition of works translated into Latin by scholars who somehow became intrigued with the process. In his *Pooh* review, Highet claims that Englishmen have been particularly susceptible to such whimsies, being fascinated by their puzzle-solving aspect.

Most of these exercises have been lost or forgotten, having served to amuse and perhaps edify a few of the select at odd moments. Probably this is only just, for they were never thought of as more than trivial entertainments, in spite of their intellectual demands.

But Glass's book is not of this sort at all, and it is in understanding the purpose behind *Washingtonii Vita,* and through that the man behind the purpose, that interests those of us who don't know Latin well enough to judge the work itself. For Glass the undertaking was one of *pietas,* an act of devotion or dutiful conduct. He did not write it as pablum (*pabulum*) for young scholars who, if they could not chew and digest Cicero, might find access to his genius through the intermediation of bloodthirsty accounts of Braddock's massacre (*Caedes Braddockiana*) or the defeat of Burgoyne (*Clades Burgoyniana*).

Glass's inspiration was far stranger and more interesting than that, for he saw in Washington a subject that was essentially Roman. This insight was not unexpected or peculiar; the emphasis upon Roman virtue and proprieties was shared by Washington's own contemporaries, and in England the literary period contemporary with his youth is designated "The Augustan Age." Furthermore, Washington's bravery, self-control, and sense of honor were thought of as ideally Roman, so that he was called "The Cincinnatus of the West," and the first great city beyond the mountains was named for him.

What could be more natural, then, than a rendering of this latter-day Roman hero's life in the language of his spiritual homeland? Dead for a quarter of a century, the Father of Our Country had already drifted to that temporal distance wherein heroism is plausible. His ill-fitting false teeth and proclivity towards port wine would suit a later age, dreary of hero worship and prurient to know the worst of all those who have been apotheosized. But for Glass's age, as for Weems's, such failure to proclaim greatness was a failure of nerve, and facts had little to do with the matter. Therefore, just as Virgil created Rome's patrimony in *The Aeneid,* connecting the known world of his day with a mythological past, so would Glass create a new image of the Father of Our Country, in a medium more suited to the heroic, emphasizing his classic virtues and rendering him a sort of *Cincinnatus Redivivus.*

A quixotic undertaking, to be sure. But Glass's life was evidently divorced from the realities of his time. Born in northern Ireland, he was brought to this country at the age of eight, and devoured the curricula given to him, so that he graduated from the University of Pennsylvania at the age of nineteen. He married young and came to Ohio in 1817, already a *paterfamilias,* and almost as unemployable in that day as he would be today. His learning was considered prodigious, and he acquired the sobriquet of "the Erasmus of the West"; but such renown was of little use on the frontier, and the rest of his life was spent in miserable poverty.

He seemed, in fact, to have a genius for impracticality and disaster. Jeremiah N. Reynolds, his friend and editor, in his introduction to Glass's *Washingtonii Vita,* states that "Glass was not deficient in mathematics and the other branches of useful science, but they were only matters of mere utility, and not of affection."

When one's sense of the useful is totally divorced from one's affection, the result is pitiful, indeed. And Reynolds's account of Glass seems a model of human loneliness and despair. "Glass," he wrote, "knew nothing of the world more than a child. He was delicately formed in mind and body, and shrunk from all coarseness as a sensitive plant from a rude touch."

Such delicacy once thrilled the bosoms of women and stirred the ambition of men. Glass died the year Byron died, and if he was hardly Byronic, he was certainly a romantic figure, according to the canons of the day, being idealistic, forlorn, morbidly sensitive, and fey, in the sense of being doomed to die young. In addition to all this, there was that spiritual exile in his being a backwoods schoolmaster in a day when such an office required and tolerated little more than physically subduing the largest, roughest student. As Reynolds politely informs the reader, "Of all the honest callings in the world, the most difficult is that of an instructor, who has to chastise idle boys, and to satisfy ignorant parents." Where is there room in such a classroom for Ciceronian eloquence? Shelley himself could have hardly fallen upon the thorns of life and bled more copiously.

Francis Glass lived an impoverished and brutal existence. Isolated and lonely, his wretchedness was total. After visiting his dwelling, Reynolds surmised that his poor friend's entire household goods "could not have been sold for the sum of thirty dollars."

But Glass's idealism was steadfast. "There were moments," his friend Reynolds says, "when hope broke in upon his despondency, and visions of glory filled his mind. He saw himself united in all coming ages with the father of his country, and with the patriotism and prowess of the greatest and the best of men, which had only been recorded in modern languages, never burning in the vernacular of Imperial Rome, nor traced with a pen plucked from the wing of the 'Mantuan Swan.' "

The irony is both understandable and complete. Latin existed unchanging and "out of time," and to the scholars of that past era, it came as close as any conceivable language to immortality.

In Peter Shaw's General Preface to his second edition (London, 1737) of Bacon's philosophical works, "Methodized, and made English, from the Originals" (ie, in Latin), Shaw analyzes Bacon's reasons for first publishing his works in Latin: they would then be available in "the most general language, that they might be read by the Men of all Nations." Also, Latin was the acknowledged language of scholarship and deemed significant of learning. Furthermore, Shaw argued, these works "have a more particular regard to Posterity, and *Latin* seems the most suitable Language for conveying things safe and unalter'd to After-Ages."

Such reasons were cogent at one time, and certainly Francis Glass believed them as fervently as Francis Bacon did. Glass and Bacon both, living two centuries apart, were in their attitudes almost equally distant from the Computer Age; and their paradoxical faith in the immortality of Latin as a living part of the world's thought, in spite of its being a dead language . . . this faith has been neither confirmed nor justified.

Still, Lord Bacon's reputation has not proved vulnerable, and he still has his place in intellectual history. But the situation is otherwise with Francis Glass, and from our vantage point today we look back and think upon the sad irony of this desperate and impoverished backwoods schoolmaster—intellectual, impractical, idealistic, and majestically ambitious—striving to be remembered after his death by writing a book in a dead language.

Somewhere, Thoreau comments that a genius is seldom encountered in this world, because it takes one to know one. Whatever its degree of truth (some products of genius are evident to everybody, even though the forces behind them remain mysterious), this principle seems to be at work in other areas often associated with genius. I speak of eccentricity, unusual convictions, and bizarre obsessions.

In terms of his immediate surroundings, Francis Glass was a crank. Generally, he was ignored, ridiculed, and misunderstood. But there was at least one exception, and this was Jeremiah N.

Reynolds, the loyal friend already referred to, who, after Glass died, worked for the publication of *Washingtonii Vita,* then edited and wrote the introduction to it. Years before, when he'd had to discontinue his studies at Ohio University, Reynolds sought out Glass so that he could continue his classical education, and this association proved to be one of the major influences upon his life.

In 1824, the year Glass died, Reynolds became editor of the Wilmington (Ohio) *Spectator.* (See *Ohio Authors and Their Books, 1796–1950,* edited by William Coyle, from which much of this information was taken.) But shortly afterwards, he fell under the influence of John Cleves Symmes, who had announced in a broadside: "I declare the earth is hollow, and habitable within, containing a number of solid concentrick spheres, one within the other, and that it is open at the poles 12 or 16 degrees."

Reynolds had a weakness for espousing the causes of other people, and took upon himself the hollow-earth theory as his own, joining Symmes on the lecture circuit and promoting various schemes for government explorations, one of which was supposed to have eventuated in the discovery of Antarctica. Reynolds obviously led an adventurous life, with "a stirring but unverified record of melodramatic action within the Arctic Circle and in the territory of the Araucanian [South American] Indians" (*Ohio Authors,* entry by Gerald D. McDonald).

When accounts of his travels and theories were published, Reynolds became a famous man. Although he was often ridiculed, his powers of persuasion were extraordinary. In 1835 (the year *Washingtonii Vita* appeared) Reynolds's *Voyage of the United States Frigate Potomac* was published, recounting the history of that ship as it explored the south seas, with Reynolds as secretary to the Commodore. After this, his passionate energy unabated, he wrote and lectured throughout the country.

Sometime during this period, his story, *Mocha Dick,* was published in the May 1839 issue of *Knickerbocker,* and it is almost certain that Herman Melville read it. It was also undoubtedly read by another famous American writer, Edgar Allan Poe, who was an admirer of Reynolds, asserting that "He has written much, and well." Poe was tangibly if indirectly influenced by Reynolds, for it was at the latter's persuasion that the United States had undertaken a naval expedition to the south polar seas, and the official report of this voyage served as the inspiration for Poe's *Narrative of Arthur Gordon Pym.*

It is odd that Reynolds could have remained so obscure. He is not listed in most standard works, and while many scholars and collectors know about *Mocha Dick,* not many seem to have read it. I was one of these until recently when I sought out a copy of the 1932 Scribner edition, illustrated by Lowell LeRoy Balcom, and read it, discovering for myself what others have presumably known or taken for granted: for all his virtues, Reynolds was not Melville, and while *Mocha Dick* is lively enough and somewhat interesting, it will remain a curiosity and little more. It seems quaint, even as it thunders: gazing upon Mocha Dick, the white whale, a man cries out, "Good heaven!"—evidently so shocked he can't even articulate the final "s" of the exclamation. Nevertheless, if only by virtue of its great subject, there are scenes and details in Reynolds's story that foreshadow that majestic cetacean whiteness lying twelve years in the future.

The reference to Poe eventually brings us back to Francis Glass, for, at the end of his *Washingtonii Vita,* there are several pages of advertisements, forerunners of today's publisher's puffs. The most interesting of these is a substantial and laudatory review from the *Southern Literary Messenger.* Although the review is unsigned, it was written by Poe, who responded feelingly to the book, in spite of initial misgivings.

> We confess that we regarded the first announcement of this *rara avis* with an evil and suspicious eye. The thing was improbable, we thought. Mr. Reynolds was quizzing us—the brothers Harper were hoaxed—and Messieurs Anthon and Co., were mistaken. At all events we had made up our minds to be especially severe upon Mr. Glass, and to put no faith in that species of classical Latin which should emanate from the backwoods of Ohio. We now solemnly make a recantation of our preconceived opinions, and so proceed immediately to do penance for our unbelief.

From here on, the review is highly favorable, and incidentally conveys the impression that Poe was intimately familiar with the texts of a more numerous population of "modern" (i.e., from Milton on) works in Latin than I have listed or even know about. Of Glass, he writes:

> His ingenuity is not less remarkable than his grammatical skill. Indeed he is never at a loss. It is nonsense to laugh at his calling Quakers *tremebundi* ["tremblers"]. *Tremebundi* is as good Latin as *trementes,* and more euphonical Latin than *Quackeri*—for both which latter ex-

pressions we have the authority of Schroeckh: and *glandes plumbeae* ["slingshot pellets of lead"], for bullets, is something better, we imagine, than Wyttenbach's *bombarda* for cannon; Milton's *globulus* ["little sphere"] for a button; or Grotius' *capilamentum* ["false hair"], for a wig.

Ideally, one should never mix an author's personality with the character of his or her work; but in fact, the honesty of reviews is often troubled by such impurities. Poe knew, liked, and respected Reynolds, through whose advocacy Glass's book had been published, and in spite of his protestations must have been somewhat well-disposed towards *Washingtonii Vita*. But I do not assume that he would have erred to the extent of perjury or that he would have concealed indifference beneath a show of enthusiasm—there are too many evasions possible to avoid hurting a friend's feelings.

And independent of his friendship for Reynolds, Poe must have keenly felt the suffering and loneliness of Glass, and would surely have admired the heroic dimensions of his accomplishment. Our personalities are structures of sorts, and each of us drops this structure like a template upon some segment of potential experience, so that what we perceive is miraculously near to what we are.

And what Poe must have seen was a forlorn genius, one who might almost have inhabited some corner of his own fiction or poetry. Even though he was married and had children, Glass was wretched in a way that could serve as an index of that older notion of "genius"—a sensitivity that was almost pathological so that even poverty, isolation, and disease were made to glow from it as rotting corpses are said to radiate a morbid glow in certain kinds of light. And even if Glass's destiny seems to be lacking in that melodrama which lies at the heart of Poe's stories, it was nonetheless an existence of passionate neglect. And although there are no ravens in Ohio, a home-grown crow might have been made to take its station somewhere in Glass's dark study, having been taught to utter a few words . . . in Latin, of course. Something like *numquam*, perhaps; which is to say, "Nevermore."

Some Letters Hiram Wrote

Except for instructions on how to close the fence gate when the latch is broken or how often to feed the cat when you're away from home, the least "literary," least self-conscious writing is to be found in the personal letters of a marginal illiterate. I'm not speaking of those casual marginal illiterates who graduated from high school or college, and take it upon themselves to write to a friend upon occasion: I'm speaking of a down-home, card-carrying illiterate who sits with his tongue between his teeth and strains over the shape of each letter as if it were a new design for a stirrup or a sword halter.

I picture Hiram Wadley writing this way. He was a cavalry soldier out west in the 1870s, and when a dozen of his letters were listed in an ad for an auction some years ago, I made certain I got there so I could have a chance to bid on them. The auctioneer had been alert enough to list these letters in the newspaper (not referring to Hiram, of course), but evidently no one took the bait, because they were knocked down to me for $1.50. All twelve of them. 12½¢ per letter: a stupendous bargain, and I still occasionally wonder why no one bid against me. Perhaps they had looked at the letters and concluded that nobody who wrote so crudely and ungrammatically would have anything worth saying.

If this was the case, the reasoning is familiar enough. We value education, and as a teacher I bear oath that we should. And yet, the ability to articulate is potentially an ability to deceive. This is old knowledge. The ancient sophists understood it, and so did Socrates, along with his antagonists. Also, there is that later saying: "Be good, young Maid, be good; and let who will be clever." Rhetoric is a fine and splendid art, but we know that it can be an insidious gift, an instrument of guile.

However, you don't have to assume any such anti-intellectual posture to savor the witnessing of an unlettered soul trying to express himself in wild and lonely surroundings. I am speaking of Hiram Wadley, whose twelve letters to his family bear witness to an earnest, responsible, unimaginative young man who lived a life of duty and action, and was obviously confined pretty much to a world of oral communication, leaving this world only upon occasion to look for his name on a sentinel roster or to carve out a message to his family.

The earliest letter, dated January 19, 1875, and written at Fort Clark, Texas, lets the reader know what he's in for. It reads as follows (page endings at breaks):

> Dear Sistors and Brother this eavng i'll write you afew lines to let you now that we are still alive and in good health this winter and hope that this will find you all well this time fore we are having very hard time now we expect to go out fore long and be gon most of the Summer but cant tell though nothing Shure of it yet we will get paid to morrow and will Send five to Emy So She can git hire Some and Tiny also fore we
>
> don't git much and ther is lots of things a Soldire need fore the (?) haf you herd from Ira Since you rote befre let me now wheather it so or not there is nothing to write about here I have been out a hunting and had a good time I run in Some wild hogs about ten of them and killed one of them and eat some fore breakfast and killed a wild of beaf or what or (?) one it had no brand on So it was ours
> I will mail this to morrow or next day as soon as they pay off
>
> this day too years I will be discharge fore or time will expire then it is along time yet dont look fore us till you See us Coming So I'll Close fore this time hoping to here from you all Soon give my love to all and Still remain your H.D. & L. Wadleigh
> oh by the way we have writing School here and ill do better next time fore my thumb is Sore I hert it last night catching ball

Well, *Caveat Lector.* Hiram Wadley (who, like Shakespeare, spelled his name three different ways,) was serving with his brother, Loren—referred to by the initial "L" in the letter just quoted. I suspect that Loren could not write at all, since Hiram never fails to include him in the general reports of events.

The letters are, by most conventional literary standards, banal, plodding, and devoid of ideas and subtlety of feeling. But as personal and historical documents, they are superbly revealing. Much can be learned about the life of the common cavalryman from this first letter out of Texas (most of the others are designated as from "Cheyenne Agency, Indian Teratory," or Fort Reno, in Wyoming). The first letter suggests that, in Texas, at least, their regimental duties were not too strict—that they could forage a little (at least kill wild hogs) and "play ball" (whatever that meant, exactly) in the evening. Other letters give interesting glimpses of life in their barracks (the only time when Hiram could write a letter), the two brothers lying on their bunks, smoking their pipes, and talking about their home back in Morgan County, Ohio, near the Muskingum River. A quite different sort of country.

Reading these letters, one begins to understand something of the life of a cavalryman in the Old West. The accumulation of facts and observations have an air of humble discovery about them: the figure of the cavalryman charging with drawn saber is a cliché of enormous recognition—a symbol. And symbols conceal reality precisely as they convey it. But Hiram is somewhere inside the symbol, and the details of the landscape there are quite different from their outer appearance. Or, indeed, invisible. In one letter, Hiram writes:

> We have got our kit gun and Sabor and belts and Dress suit ti i have more brass to (clean) than it would take to make a house i can do it eny how we had to a monthly in spection to day. there is lots of them read men out here wher i am but they are now still at presant but dont now how long they will be ther is about a thousand camp in Sight of us now

"i can do it eny how," Hiram Wadley says, speaking of the harsh discipline of soldiering in those days, and there is no evidence to contradict this truth. He was a solid soldier and reported on the life around him as he saw it.

Certain themes preoccupy him: he misses girls (although later, we find out he's turned against them because of some unfortunate business, and will satisfy himself with "squarse"—as if they weren't "girls" but simply female Indians) and asks for the name of one he can write to. There are numerous references to money transactions, most of which make little sense out of the context of the letters Hiram is answering. Although there is one purchase that

looms in his imagination—a pocket watch, Victorian symbol of af-
fluence and gentility (not to mention a businesslike access to the
"right" time):

> well you where saying Some thin a bout $21 dolars i dont mind if eny
> thing of that kind i where thinking Some of Sending after a watch if
> you think you will go to Athens i witch you would get me one ill tell
> you what to do it you havent put thet $25 d away So it will be eny
> bothere to get it witch you would get me one ore give it to ER King if
> you haven't time to go to Athens don't go to eny truble about it fore it
> wont pay if you have it and dont want to   (?) it get me one ori
> give it to E.R. and he will Send

> me one from Chilcothe if you I give it to him tell him what it is fore i
> dont want it Stored after first fo febrary fore i think we will move in
> the Spring and i dont want it Stored after then if we Stay her next
> Summer . . .

And so forth. The laboring over the purchase and care of this watch
is impressive in view of Hiram's difficulty in writing, the general
shortage of writing supplies, and the risks in sending mail out of
Indian Territory all the way back east and down into a tiny, rough
Appalachian township. (All turns out well, however; after a long
delay, the watch is bought, mailed, and arrives safely.)

Such fragments of personal details fired my curiosity about
Hiram Wadley, so I wrote to the National Archives, requesting information about him and his brother. The answer was prompt and,
in its limited way, informative. The brothers had enlisted on January 19, 1875; their occupation: miners; birthplace, Morgan County,
Ohio. Hiram was 21 years old, 5'8" tall, with brown hair, brown
eyes, and "ruddy" complexion. (He was stocky; in one of his letters
he mentioned that he weighed 180 pounds.) Loren was two years
older, an inch shorter, with blue eyes—but otherwise described as
the same. Both boys were in the 4th Cavalry Regiment, Co. L.
Hiram was mustered out in 1881, with an "excellent" character
reference. Loren received a medical discharge the same year, suffering from "Inflammation of the Lungs." (The man next in line on
the page, named Wilson, was reported to have deserted in 1876.)

After a brief search, I was able to find a history of the 4th Cavalry,
but the information seemed a rather dull accumulation of rather
dull facts, and I got the impression that—through no fault of their
own, no doubt—the 4th Cavalry was a somewhat less than colorful
outfit. And yet, being in "Indian Territory" in those days was an

adventure simply in itself, in *being* there, in a cavalry uniform; and you don't have to be a sentimentalist or too hopeless a romantic to feel the great breathtaking openness, power, and mystery of that dark and windy land in those days.

Of course, back of most of it were the Indians (Hiram never wrote "Injins," which is not the miracle of his spelling "Cheyenne" correctly, but close to it). His letter from Fort Reno, Wyoming, on June 9, 1876,[1] reveals something of the pitch of excitement all the men lived under. After stating that he is in good health, he goes on to say:

the other eaving when i was a fraid of my Self fore there was a great Ster in Camp that night ill tell you how it is i am detail to work on the sawmill over

in town so we stay ther and draw our rasions ther is three of us we was down to the store that eaving and just come back to mill at dusk and we saw the amlance go by and the was the officer in it and came our lieutenant and his his (?) and his orderly with him so we thought there was Something up and we looked around the corner of the mill and there was 25 men mouned ["mounted"] and redy to make a dash in no time if they herd Shot i went up to them and they new nothing of what was up and then the orderly came back and then they all went down to the indian camp and they resed five chief cut fingar big mouth, Wherlwind and big cow

took them up to our camp and put them in the gardhous the caus of this was that white hair a cheaif and one other indian kill the doctor son a year a go and they just came back to camp and they could not find them and they took thoes fellows till the rest of them would bring him in and the next day they held a councill of war and fetched in the murders so they are in the arms now and ever things is still but they men of our company was redy fore a fight if they hadent of give him up . . .

The evidence of such passages seems to me suggestive of something profound that I can't quite define, and oddly poetic in its attempt to somehow make the memory of that evening's violent confusion fit into the unfamiliar shapes of words upon a page.

It is evident that the "school" Hiram referred to in his first letter was not of much help in taming his language into a more conven-

1. After this essay was published in *The Ohio Magazine*, a history buff wrote to say that Fort Reno was not operative at this date. This is curious, indeed; but I think I'll believe Hiram—his spelling was majestically erratic, but I think he probably knew where he was most of the time.

tional behavior. So far as this body of evidence is concerned, his spelling remained stoutly invulnerable to whatever attempts were made to improve it. Instead of looking into his heart to write, Hiram listened to his ear.

Nowhere is this more evident than in his letter of July 14, 1876, which contains what is probably the strangest, perhaps in its way the most grotesque, report ever written of one of the famous episodes in American history. I will quote it entire, from the beginning:

> Deare Sisters and Brother
> as I will pen you a few line this morning to inform that botha of us well hoping that it will find you all well also to you want to the newes i will give all i now that indian was takin to Sill and i hant herd waht hase be come of him there has been a grat masacrea up in the black hill this last month there was a holl masacrea this time
>
> Gen McCuskey was kill and 15 officer and three hunared men a about 320 men all to geather the sues indian up a about 2500 all told and Gen McCuskey run on them with three Company and the Sues serround him and all of thes men an killed all of them and dinted have one to tell the tale as been herd of yet that was the worst slaughter was herd of yet of the indian so i gess it so but i think that Some of our rigment will go it that is so i think it will be my Company if there is eny of them goes and then will see the panted rascal there if are running (?) men in there all the time
>
> i dont care a bout going So very bad if they want to give ("go"?) them i am that Kind of a man now dont care where i am So it is where there is now girls i don't like them_____very much now if i did would stade ther with them they haf all went back on me So i will _____ Spite them by Staying here fare a while where there is lots of Squarse is so i Cant think of eny more at presant So i will quite So from your humble Servant Hiram Wadley to his friend David and Sisters _____ (?) by
>
> you can Send my pickure fore Loren

Hiram Wadly
Co I 4 U.S.Cavy.
I.T.

> Fort Reno
> Co I. 4 Reg. US
> Cavelry
>   Ind Territory

Custer was a famous general, even in his own time, and it is curious that Hiram Wadley somehow made "McCuskey" out of the name of so celebrated and controversial a man as his fellow Ohioan.

Fort Reno was not far from the scene of the massacre near the Little Bighorn, and probably all of the cavalrymen of the 4th expected to be called out at a moment's notice. Assuming that Hiram wrote this letter shortly after hearing the news, one is impressed by the fact that it had evidently taken almost three weeks to reach his post. It is hard for us to understand what life was like in such a world, insulated from relatively near events, so that news traveled circuitously and haphazardly, at the rate of a trotting horse or a riverboat.

But Hiram Wadley has left some evidence of what it must have been like to experience that world through the eyes and ears of that most difficult of abstractions, "the Common Man." I can't help but wonder about him: did he return to Morgan County and go back down into the deep mines for coal? Did he raise a family and tell them stories about the Indians and his "rigment"? If he did, I imagine he left out details about the "lots of Squarse" he'd gotten to know; but then, he may have grown into a cantankerous and outspoken old man, no more capable of being domesticated in Victorian manners than by conventions of spelling and syntax.

These are questions beyond conjecture, since I've come upon no further evidence that Hiram Wadley ever existed, even for a moment, upon this earth. It is futile to look for his name in local histories and records, although I *have* looked, of course. But he is not the sort of man who will likely be found listed among Members of the Bar, Local Bankers, Politicians, or other Leaders.

So, like the overwhelming majority of all who have lived on this earth, he appears to have been expendable in the extreme, and in one view it could be argued that he might just as well never have existed. The scanty evidence of this thin packet of letters does not suggest that he had even "killed an Indian."

But I am curious about him and interested. I've experienced something of his humanity through letters that were written privately to his sisters and brothers. I know something about him; have even gotten to know him a little, and after all this time, such curiosity is hardly an invasion of privacy.

As for the mystery of this ignorant boy's life, there is all that anyone could wish to contemplate. One of the things that bothers me is, I don't even know how to pronounce his name: does it rhyme with "badly," "godly," or "staidly"?

Maybe if I ever come upon somebody with that name I'll find out.[2] Or at least get a pretty good idea, even if whoever it is doesn't have any connection whatsoever with Morgan County, Ohio, and doesn't have any more idea of what his great-great grandfather was about than, well, the average person does.

2. I now have. Shortly after this was first printed, David Wadley (rhyming with "godly") phoned, saying that he thought he was probably distantly related to Hiram. David Wadley is a school teacher in Morgan County and has traced his family history with great care, and the connection is almost certain. He showed me a copy of the 1860 census, listing Loren and Hiram as seven and five years old, respectively. So Hiram was about twenty-two or twenty-three when he wrote these letters.

The Courage to Be Original and the Expanding Universe of Collectibles

**W**hat this particular universe turns upon is the instinct to gather and order objects, all in their various orbits, around a single idea. It is a powerful and fundamentally healthy instinct, maligned by the simple-minded cant of "anal retention," and yet corruptible into a vivid and specific form of madness.

In the world of rare books, such madness is often colorful. Sir Thomas Phillipps had it, admitted to being a "vellomaniac," and packed entire rooms of his great country houses with books and then sealed them off. Richard Heber was riddled with it and owned whole libraries in London, Oxford, Paris, Antwerp, Ghent, Hodnet (*Hodnet?* A small village in Shropshire), and still other places. Heber is said to have spent over £180,000 upon his books, in a day when one could live comfortably, if humbly, on £100 a year. Translating into today's dollars, this would compute to something like twenty to thirty million dollars, but in "real" spending power (a difficult and necessarily vague abstraction, variable according to what the money is spent *for*), the amount in most transactional contexts would prove to be much greater.

The United States has had its share of bibliocentrics in the grand tradition. As is the case with their mad English cousins, listing even a fair sampling of these would take too long. To understand something of the degree and intensity of the epidemic, however, you might go to Carl L. Cannon's *American Book Collectors and Collecting: From Colonial Times to the Present* (the "present" being 1941, when the book was first published in New York). Also, there are such rich repositories of fact and anecdote as Charles Everitt's *The Adventures of a Treasure Hunter* (Boston, 1952) and Donald Bower's

Fred Rosenstock: A Legend in Books and Art (np, 1976). (The list could be extended; these are a mere sampling of the genre.)

But one entry from Cannon's book will provide an instance of the progress of the disease. Cannon's subject is the great historian, Bancroft. "Far western history was a virgin field when young Hubert Howe Bancroft arrived in California in 1852," we are informed. Later, when Bancroft established the "mercantile and publishing house that bore his name," he began, for research purposes, to buy all the books he could find on California.

Soon, he was visiting bookshops wherever he traveled, and he traveled extensively. The symptoms of his eventual and total transformation into a great collector became increasingly evident. Cannon quotes from Bancroft's memoirs, titled *Literary Industries:*

> Old, rare, and valuable books would increase rather than diminish in value, and as I came upon them from time to time I thought it best to secure all there were relating to this [California] coast. After all the cost in money was not much; it was the time that counted; and the time, might it not be as profitable so spent as in sipping sugared water on the Paris boulevard?[1]

By now, Bancroft's passion was thoroughly aroused, and he worked relentlessly at buying—often for dimes and quarters—everything relating to his subject: pamphlets, letters, documents, broadsides, and especially books:

> I did not stop to consider, I did not care, whether the book was of any value or not; it was easier to buy it than to spend time in examining its value. Besides, in making such a collection it is impossible to determine . . . what is of value and what is not.[2]

Here we are on the verge, no doubt: but what a lovely prospect that verge affords! This madness is like no other, and even its most obviously pathological symptoms are not devoid of a sort of grace.

Spinoza's Dutch contemporaries gave him the epithet, *Gotbetrunken*—"God drunk"—and in a similar way, the most radical bibliocentrics may be thought of as *Bokbetrunken*. In this conceit one may contemplate the fact that the book, as the ultimate vessel of revelation and truth, is the mystic symbol of both obsessions.

---

1. *American Book Collectors,* p. 97.
2. Ibid.

The desire simply to possess, though essential, is only a part of collecting rare books. Fulfillment or realization of the ideal requires a counter passion, that of ordering, of arranging, of "making sense" out of the marvelous variety implicit in any sizable accumulation of books. There is a pleasure in taxonomy analogous to the pleasures of music.

And yet, in the universe of books, the class of old and established rarities is, after all, something of a closed system. The likelihood of a Bay Psalm Book appearing in some slush of old volumes is constantly diminishing with the years, even though no one can say for sure that there is no unknown copy existing in some trunk in an attic or box in a shed. There are a lot of books moldering away in forgotten and half-forgotten places; and the chances of a copy of the Bay Psalm Book turning up can be plotted as a hyperbolic curve, descending relentlessly with the years, ever approaching the straight line of the impossible asymptote without ever quite touching it.

Such breathtaking rarity would discourage even the hardest bibliophile, if these were the only sorts of books worth collecting. In this case, not even madness would help. And for someone with "limited funds" (as the euphemistic cliché has it; I'm speaking of poor folks, here), the situation would be even more obviously desperate.

Salvation comes in the form of the wonderful plenitude of books that are available, and within this abundance still another of books that are not merely available, but worth collecting. In short, the realm of collectible books is constantly expanding . . . not merely through a willing suspension of disbelief, to soothe the feverish need to collect, but *intrinsically,* in terms of the real and intelligent need that such books can serve.

In the United States alone, something like 100 books are printed every day. Most of these are nonbooks—specialized technical reports, house organ spin-offs, promotional and advertising publications, and so forth. Of the remainder, however, it is in the nature of things that the majority will not prove successful by any criterion: they will not sell enough copies to pay their own production costs, nor will they prove to be a critical success. Why are these books published, then, if the chances are so slight?

A good question, best answered with reference to various proportions of human gullibility, idealism, understanding of the unpredictability of public taste, and a faint, sly realization that one best-seller might subsidize a score, or even a hundred, lesser books (in terms of sales), and that genuine literary merit is at least as likely, and possibly much more likely, to appear in the class of medium sellers than in the class of best-sellers. Yes, it is possible that there are still vestiges of responsibility and a commitment to literary values among the goliaths of publishing, no matter how much you hear about conglomerate takeovers and the subsequent decline of any policy incompatible with the most stupid application of the doctrine of the bottom line.

But here we are talking about "collectible" books. There is nothing intrinsically wrong or silly in collecting best-sellers, providing you feel strongly about them and know what you're doing. Knowing what you're doing *usually* means knowing how to identify a first edition; but this isn't necessarily the case. I can't imagine why, but there just might be people who collect book club editions—seek them out and rejoice in them. Their rationalizations must be cunning, and I would like to know what they are, other than the simple, plain, dumb, relentless availability of the object of their chase. But rarity, or at least scarcity, provides much of the interest in collecting; so that to collect book club editions would be a little like a hunter specializing in shooting spaniels or house cats.

Of course, despised books suffer the consequences of contempt and evaporate with what is at times astonishing rapidity (not rapid enough for those book club copies of *Captain from Castile* and *The Carpetbaggers,* however), and the eventual scarcity of such books can provide one of the conditions for a legitimate market. Think of Big Little Books and the Armed Forces editions of WW II.

Collectibility is in itself irrelevant to the publication of most books; and yet this fact does not necessarily mean that some titles from this class of book are *not* collectible. Josiah Gregg's *Commerce of the Prairies* (New York, 1844), was not brought out as a future collectible. I doubt if such a thought troubled the publishers—even though the first edition is a handsome as well as sturdy product. It was made to last and be used; the title conveys the utilitarian character of Gregg's book; and it succeeded well, in addition to the fact of becoming a most desirable Americana title all these years later, worth $500 and more in its first edition.

Other books are published as instant collectibles, and today these provide a rich harvest for the collector with patience, taste, and a little money to spend. I am speaking of the private presses that are flourishing throughout the country, along with the new young typographers whose pamphlets and broadsides are often priced as works of art . . . some of them deservedly. Such collecting can be inexpensive, or it may not be: broadsides and small pamphlets (numbered and signed by the artist, poet, and typographer, for example) sometimes cost in the hundreds, but others can be bought for much less. Read what Bob Hayman has to say on the subject:

> Every bookseller, collector and librarian—unless he or she has been asleep for twenty years—is aware of the massive proliferation of private presses in recent years. Actually, there is nothing new about it but it seems to have gotten out of control now. There is nothing intrinsically wrong with printing new books but I do have great objections to the pricing policies of some of these printers and publishers. If you read many dealers' catalogues it will not take you long to find examples. One favorite ploy is to take the poetry of some fellow most of us have never heard of—poetry sometimes sprinkled with four-letter words—print it in a small edition, perhaps have the poet sign it, then sock a fancy price tag of perhaps several hundred dollars on it. In my opinion this type of book is strictly a ripoff.
>
> Fortunately, not all private presses operate this way, which brings me directly to the private press of John Cumming, some of whose productions are offered here. From his press at Mount Pleasant, Michigan, has come a steady stream of solid historical works, beautifully printed and bound, all in small limited editions, and all at reasonable prices. In my opinion he is making a great contribution to the literature of American history and in the process also producing beautiful books. Judge for yourself.

This panegyric is on page 19 of Hayman's Catalogue #89, Spring, 1982, and after it he lists ten titles from Cumming's press. Who could resist? I couldn't, and ordered two of them—George Burges's *A Journal of a Surveying Trip into Western Pennsylvania . . . in the Year 1795* and John Gates Thurston's *A Journal of a Trip to Illinois in 1836*. Their price? $12.50 and $10.00. Furthermore, all ten titles Hayman listed are limited to less than 500, and they contain primary source material, even though some of them have just been published after sulking for almost two centuries in the vats of old records or diaries.

The books are, as Hayman claimed, handsomely printed. Cumming's introduction to Thurston's account ends with a flourish:

> Since this journal is presented on its own merits and as an exercise in typography the editor, printer, and publisher all agree with himself that it is not necessary to burden this book with footnotes and explanations. The hand-setting of type encourages economy of words.

In that last sentence, Cumming exemplifies the truth expressed, reminding one that, for reasons not totally dissimilar, typographical errors are seldom found on the headstones of graves.

Beyond doubt, some private press titles will, more or less consistently, prove good investments; although this fact, here as elsewhere, should be secondary to an honest appreciation of the work itself as an object of literary, historical, or artistic merit.

As we liberate ourselves from old prejudices (not all indefensible, if the truth be told), we learn to appreciate new sorts of books to collect. This expanding universe is not precisely measurable, of course, but it is clearly identifiable. Thirty years ago, collecting science fiction or fantasy or popular detective fiction was clearly eccentric. Now, these subjects have entered the mainstream of collecting, and the auction and dealer track records of a first edition copy of *Tarzan of the Apes* or the first edition of Haggard's *Dawn* or *The Maltese Falcon* are pretty clearly established.

With imagination and honest attentiveness (do you *really* like the work of a certain author, or are you merely taking your cue from others?), you will settle upon something that is precisely to your taste as a collector; and the beauty of this is, if you can't afford to spend lavishly, you can still collect some sort of book worth collecting. In fact, if you have a little time and use of a car (although I recently heard of an active collector/dealer in Chicago who operates without owning a car) and a *little* money, you can collect simply, intelligently, and satisfyingly.

How much is "a little money"? Well, you name it. There are potentially and theoretically collectible books that can be had for practically nothing. Consider early automobile tour guides: they are everywhere, and yet they are fascinating and important documents of Americana. They contain information about a phase of our history that has changed American life radically. We'll never be the same. Look at a 1928 AAA Tour Book and study the map of Cleveland in it, or St. Louis, or San Francisco. That map will show a place, a city, a world that did not exist before and will never return. Read the text; think of the sort of life that is symbolized and figured forth by all that is contained in that black or dark dullgreen, limp imitation-leather volume.

And what will you have to pay for such a marvel? A quarter, perhaps. A dime. Maybe fifty cents. I have come upon many, never fail to pick them up (now, that is; for a long time I ignored them, like just about everybody else), and have only recently begun to see an occasional title priced as a desirable, salable book.

There are whole classes of books that are simply ignored and should not be. Why should they not be? Because, in their own ways, they convey a special, unique sense of the culture they came out of—and through that, of the human situation.

Consider children's books, boys' books. The once-popular novels of Robert Ballantyne, Oliver Optic, Jacob Abbot (The "Rollo" series), G. A. Henty, James Otis, Capt. Mayne Reid, and a hundred other authors are found everywhere. Some are even in good condition and may be picked up for a dollar or two each. These boy novels are often predictably about cowboys and Indians (in which case, they merge naturally and gracefully into other collecting areas: Americana and popular culture studies), but sometimes they are about new technology (e.g., the "Radio Boys" and "the Motorboat Boys" series). Though cheaply made, these are often interesting and attractive books in good condition, with bright pictorial bindings.

I am here referring to "middle-aged" children's books; and while I have listed only a few of the boys' books, there are at least as many girls' books of the same general type, directed towards the same age levels, as the titles of Caroline Keene ("Nancy Drew") and Laura Hope ("the Bobbsey Twins")—but these authors are already being collected, and prices for first editions are soaring into the rarified regions of the first editions of the Oz books, and even higher to, say, those of Beatrix Potter.

Pictorial bindings themselves can be exquisite, and there is no reason that people couldn't collect books as simple art objects—for their lavish and colorful bindings. Part of me rebels against this; my own prejudice is that a book is an instrument for reading, and the act of reading—not looking at illustrations or palpating leather bindings—should be the living heart of all collecting. Nevertheless, there is nothing wrong with someone collecting one class of books for their physical attractiveness—illustrated nineteenth-century editions of fairy tales, for example—and another class for reading: the first editions of Trollope and Henry James, for example.

Books printed near the turn of the century, featuring Gibson girl covers and frontispieces (often by the legion of Gibson's imitators) are easily and cheaply available . . . although you will have to pay for such a special production as *The Gibson Book* (New York, 1906), an oblong folio in two volumes that will sell for well over $100.

Colored pictorial bindings are vivid and sprightly artifacts, conveying the sense of a past time. Antique collectors should find them indispensable, if they collect in that period; they should, but most do not. At least, not yet; but I think that surely the time will come. A lavishly decorated binding in fine bright condition is at least as worthy an art object as a Weller vase, or print or other wall decoration. It almost seems foolish to have to point this out; and yet, the point needs making.

Literary collectibles are everywhere, and a surprisingly large number of contemporary authors bring out titles that soon appear in dealers' catalogues, marked at premium prices for first edition copies. These authors also have signed limited editions of (usually smaller) works printed by private presses and trade publishers both. It is pleasurable and sensible to collect the works of a living author; furthermore, most writers are not the snarling fear biters of legend, and are easily approachable (at writers' conferences, autograph parties, public readings) for an autograph or inscription on the fly leaf of one of their books.

Aside from these more-or-less canonized writers, however, there are others who are largely unknown; and such writers provide a wonderful opportunity for the attentive reader who wants to collect. One of the finest novelists, essayists, and "persons-of-letters" now living is a Canadian, Robertson Davies. I think he is a wise and gifted writer; and yet it seems that few literate people in the United States know about his work. Certainly, there is no stigma to his "being a Canadian"; but I can't help thinking that, bearing this label, Davies pays a price in being tacitly ignored as somehow irrelevant or—even worse—regional. (The fact that Joyce and Faulkner were both regional writers does nothing to erase the smudge of contempt in the label.)

The market of collectibles expands in two ways, as I've indicated: through the increasing production of books year by year and through newly developed interests in books that have always been more or less available, but have never excited particular interest.

The next sort of uncollected collectible I would like to write about relates more or less to the latter group; and it will require courage to risk the scorn and contempt of old-fashioned dedicated collectors by uttering the heresies I'm about to utter; but fancy, if not truth, must be served.

My particular fancy is that the time will come—and *should*

come—when rebound books will be accepted in one's own personal collection, and—even more heretical—that *ex libris* books, with all their disgusting maculations of black print and Dewey decimal numbers sealed in white, ineradicable ink on the spines, will also find their place in collecting.

Here, I am not speaking of a third edition copy of *In Cold Blood,* stamped and pocketed by the Tacoma, Washington, public library . . . nor am I speaking of a first edition copy, so marked. Contemporary books are too common for any serious collector to forgive such blemishes in a copy.

And yet, even here there can be rare exceptions. I have a disgustingly worn book club edition of Saul Bellow's *Herzog.* Library pocket on the front fly leaf, Scotch tape staining the front pastedown with amber strips, where it has been applied to seal down the plastic-covered dust jacket. On the pastedown is printed: "The John McIntire Public Library, Zanesville, Ohio." Also, clearly stamped upon it is the word "Withdrawn." Very proper; very depressing.

I bought this copy from a junk store in McConnelsville, Ohio, about forty miles down the Muskingum River from Zanesville. Why did I buy it? Because of a postcard inserted, dated November 14, 1964. It reads:

Dear Mrs._____:

I am sorry to say that all speculations are baseless. I simply borrowed Zanesville for my own purposes. An old friend of mine, Robert Hivnor, talks of Zanesville continually, and the name simply lodged in my brain. Evidently my unconscious mind did the rest.

Sincerely yours,

(signed) Saul Bellow

This is, of course, a delightful association copy, and it is appropriate that the ex lib copy itself house that short courteous note from the author. No first edition in mint condition would do: here, this specific ex lib copy is required, bearing the date of the Zanesville Public Library.

The fact that the book was eventually discarded and sold is unfortunate, in a way, but not necessarily indicative of insensitivity on the part of the librarian (who had evidently read *Herzog,* liked it, and written to satisfy her curiosity about the reference to Zanesville in it); the lives of librarians are difficult enough without holding them responsible for the disposition of discarded books in weeding

. . . even though it might seem that this particular copy should have been preserved in something like a Special Collection room.

However, most small city libraries don't have special collections, and don't have the facilities for harboring even such interesting association items as this. Nevertheless, one can't help wondering if perhaps the book would not have joined the twenty-five cent discards in one of the library's sales if Bellow's response had been positive, and he'd written lyrically about a visit to Zanesville in some far distant past, when he met a girl named Judy, who . . . Well, such speculations don't clear our heads, and there's no point in dwelling upon them.

The prohibition against *ex libris* books is not absolute. To object to ex lib stamps or markings in a sixteenth- or seventeenth-century book, indicating that it was once part of a monastery library or perhaps the private library of a nobleman, is overly fastidious. Such marks convey part of the history of that copy and enrich it, even if the monastary has no particular relevance to the subject matter or if the duke who owned it played no particular role in history.

While old ex lib markings on books may be tolerable, part of their interest and value, even . . . modern public library marks are viewed through an entirely different lens. Like most collectors of modest resources I have labored long and carefully over the tasks of removing white ink acquisition numbers from the spines of otherwise valuable books and removing glued spine labels (on leather books, don't steam: apply water carefully to dissolve the paper, then rub the label off and treat the leather).

But why isn't an early twentieth-century library stamp as much a part of a copy's history as those early marks from a monastery or private collection? A book's provenance is not limited to its origin, but includes all of its previous history, so that one might cherish the evidence of a book's travels through time, with three or four library stamps showing traces of its ownership at different periods.

And yet, we do make distinctions, and can't help ourselves, even if we are able to justify *ex libris* marks and labels theoretically. Collecting old and rare books is not a totally theoretical enterprise, for the impulse behind it is a matter of feeling, as well, along with a dash of superstition and magic.

Thus it is that my 1715 London edition of *The Theological Works of the Honourable Robert Boyle, Esq: Epitomized,* by Richard Boulton, "late of Brazen-Nose College in Oxford," is marred by the black stamp of the College of Wooster, along with the thick-lettered

WITHDRAWN slanting across the page directly underneath "epito-mized." But this is a marvelous book, and I cherish it, stigmata and all. The author is *the* Robert Boyle, one of the great founders of modern science and the eponym of Boyle's Law. That so distinguished a scientist should prove a masterful prose stylist is hardly miraculous, but it is worthy of our admiration.

Boyle's gift with language centered upon his ability to provide homely examples for lofty ideas—very much in the manner of the time, but with more vivid effect than most. The following passage conveys his own method while ostensibly directed toward spiritual improvement, thus comprising its own point as it expresses it:

> But the Use of Occasional Reflections does not only learn us Attention in considering what occurs, and to reflect on them seriously as well as to express them fitly, but also teaches us how to make those Objects informative; For either by Example, Analogy or some other way, we are led to the Discovery of several Useful Notions, especially Practical Ones, and indeed the World is a Book of the God of Nature, full of Instructive Lessons, had we Skill, and would we take pains to pick them out. The Creatures are Hyerogliphicks, which contain the Mysterious Secrets of Knowledge and Piety. And as Chymists boast of an Elyxir, which might turn the worst of Metals into Gold, so Wisdom enriches the Possessor of it with useful and pretious Thoughts; and as a good Husbandman can enrich the ground, and promote the Growth of useful grains, as well as the most flagrant [*sic*] flowers by so abject a thing as Dung; a Wise Man may improve the Noblest Faculties of the Soul, and the Loveliest Qualities of the Mind, by the meanest Creatures and the slightest Objects.

And the loveliest qualities of this noble thought have been embodied in the lowest image of dung, precisely as the passage itself argues. Q.E.D.

This volume is bound in contemporary, paneled, blind-stamped calf, and it is predictably broken at the hinges. Whether I should have it rebacked is a troublesome question, in view of that damaged title page. Eventually, I'll probably have it repaired, for, as the quoted sample should demonstrate, Boyle's gifts were not limited to chemistry; and reading his words as they were gathered in Boulton's "epitomized" edition, within a generation of Boyle's death, carries the full luster of his thinking, even to the quaint archaism in the word "learn"—meaning then to teach, but retained in our day only by the most stubborn and ignorant speakers from the darkest backwoods, hills, and swamps of the language.

The realm of uncollected collectibles expands coincidentally with the past and with the diversification of books. And while it is true that someone whose budget is severely limited may have to compromise, that compromise does not have to deserve the epithet "base"; but may, rather, be the sort of compromise that is essential for enlightenment and civilization itself. It may, at best, be a triumph of imagination.

Consider old bound volumes of periodicals. There are multitudes of them, and most are bought by antique dealers and others whose ideal is *Godey's Lady's Book,* with its color illustrations showing female attire. Very nice, beyond doubt; but such bound periodicals have bigger fish in them for those with literary taste, and if your collecting is literary, you won't have to compete with the *Godey's* buyers, whose enthusiasm drives prices up.

I am speaking of bound periodicals with first printings of great writers in them. These can be had for next to nothing. I recently bought a bound volume of *The United States Magazine and Democratic Review,* vol. XIV (New York, 1844). I paid $5 for it, and the man who sold it to me probably knew that Hawthorne had contributed three stories this particular year. The fact is explicit in the table of contents. However, bound periodicals are simply not sought after. But for the lover of Hawthorne's works, his contributions to periodicals and other publications (Merle Johnson states that such gift annuals as *The Token* "practically supported Hawthorne up to the time of 'The Twice Told Tales' ") provide a fascinating and convenient way of collecting his true "first editions" at only a fraction of the cost of a first edition of *The Scarlet Letter* alone.

Collecting an author's contributions to periodicals is often a challenge to one's simple grasp of facts—the bibliography of that author. If you come upon a bound copy of *Putnam's Monthly Magazine,* vol. IV, covering July to December, 1854, buy it, for it contains the first six installments of Melville's novel Israel Potter. But since the piece is unsigned, only those who know mid-nineteenth-century literature will identify this first appearance of Melville's least-known novel. Even fewer will know that the short story in the same volume, "The Lightning Rod Man," is also by Melville. Contributions by famous authors were often unsigned in early times, and this is one reason that such bound volumes are so common and so cheap in price.

Various sorts of technical books are waiting to be collected. There is a limbo that medical, legal, and scientific books fall into, when they are too old to be relevant and not old enough to be interesting for antiquarian reasons. But "not old enough" is a relative judgment that needs constantly to be renegotiated, especially in the contexts of burgeoning technology. The vanguard of the "Antiquarian" moves forward relentlessly. Practically anybody will surmise that a medical book from the eighteenth century or a seventeenth-century legal tome has intrinsic collectors' interest, but what about early nineteenth-century books? If they have plates, medical books from this period are worth having, and are not all that scarce or expensive. If the plates are hand colored, all the better.

Similarly, legal books from 1800 to 1850 can be fascinating, for they provide a glimpse into considered and controversial issues of the day, and contain important and at times absorbing information about a past time, when steamboats were still new and required interpretation according to the law, as did canal boats and stage coaches, which carried, along with goods and people, all the problems consequent upon the accumulation of goods and people everywhere, at any time, as modified by the technology of those times and places. Old legal books can be hard reading for the layman, but with patience and close attention, a reader can find his way through the legalese and trumpery of ceremonious diction to the stories at their heart—tales of greed, passion, cunning, and remorse.

We live in the neck of an hourglass, braced by the twin mysteries of Future and Past. It is natural, but an impoverishment, that most of us spend virtually all of our energies upon this brief and evanescent interval of time. That the Present should occupy us is necessary, of course; we have no real alternative. But it is not essential that our imaginations should be so confined. We relate to the Present and prepare for the Future, trying as we do so to shape it by modulating the flow of time through the hours, days, and minutes that we can feel and touch. And yet, it is important that we relate to the Past, as well; and the Past comes to us largely, and sometimes most intimately, through books.

Even a recently published science fiction novel, whose events are supposed to transpire at some awesomely distant future date . . . even this comes to us from the Past. It comes to us in the form of a book—something set up and proofread and printed months before—and the time of its origin is in some ways as distant as the world of Chaucer and Jonathan Swift, for the Past contains as many mysteries as the Future, and the book is its vessel.

Jack Matthews has collected old and rare books for many years, and currently he and his wife, Barbara, buy, sell, and trade first editions, antiquarian books, and old Americana (including early manuscript diaries, journals, broadsides, steamboat logs, and Indian Americana). Many of their books are stored in an old defunct saloon, bought for that purpose and located in a small, southeastern Ohio mining town.

Matthews is Distinguished Professor of English at Ohio University, in Athens, Ohio.

The Johns Hopkins University Press

BOOKING IN THE HEARTLAND

This book was composed in Garth Graphic by BG Composition, Inc., from a design by Martha Farlow. It was printed on 50-lb. Sebago Eggshell Cream Offset paper and bound in Holliston's Roxite B and Kingston Natural with Multicolor Antique end sheets by the Maple Press Company.